FAMILIAR STRANGER

A HENSON SERIES NOVEL

DARA GIRARD

ISBN 13: 978-1949764178

FAMILIAR STRANGER

ILORI PRESS BOOKS, LLC

PO Box #10332

Silver Spring, MD 20914

www.iloripressbooks.com

The Black Stockings Society

Power Play

A Gentleman's Offer

Body Chemistry

Round the Clock

Return of the Black Stockings Society

Playing for Keeps

After Hours

A Private Affair

Just One Look

Private Lessons

Henson Series

Table for Two

Familiar Stranger

Gaining Interest

Careless Rapture

Dangerous Curves

Duvall Sisters

The Glass Slipper Project

Taming Mariella

A Reluctant Hero

The Clifton Sisters

The Sapphire Pendant

The Amber Stone

The Emerald Ring

It Happened One Wedding

Unexpected Pleasure

Midnight Promise

Sweet Temptation

Always and Forever

Truly Yours

Novels

Illusive Flame

Honest Betrayal

The Daughters of Winston Barnett

Remember My Name

She was officially back in hell. All because she'd taken the advice of her seventy-eight year old grandmother. Greta Rodgers resisted the urge to bang her head against the wall as she hid inside a toilet stall in her old high school. It was reasonably clean but she still didn't want to touch anything. She'd spent plenty of time in the stalls, between classrooms, to get away from the gauntlet of taunts that usually greeted her in the hallway. The jocks and cheerleaders had been her biggest tormentors—trying their best to flaunt their position of power at the top of the high school food chain. Why had she come back? Greta shook her head. She already knew the answer: Her grandmother had insisted and she always liked to please her.

"You should go," her grandmother had said when Greta had confided in her about her upcoming twenty year high school reunion. They sat in her grandmother's private room, in the senior resident apartment where she lived. The room was spotless with a small side table, placed directly under the window, displaying a porcelain tea set, which they never used.

Her grandmother just liked it for decoration. Her grandmother, who she affectionately called 'Minnie', wasn't an imposing figure, but looked like she could be, if she wanted to. She was a very attractive woman who always dressed well, although throughout her life she'd never made the income to equal her finer tastes. She'd been born in Jamaica, and had fallen in love with, and married, an African American who was visiting the island on business. She had come to the States in her early twenties. Within four years she'd had three children, gained a new life, and lost her husband to an au pair from Belgium he had met on one of his business trips. When he disappeared, instead of returning to her family in Jamaica, she stayed and worked several odd jobs, to support her family. Greta greatly admired Minnie and used her experience as an immigrant as a constant source of inspiration.

"But I don't like reunions," Greta said. "Because I don't believe in rehashing the past."

"I've enjoyed every reunion I've gone to."

Greta grinned. "You've never gone to a reunion."

"I would have enjoyed myself if I had." She laughed.

No doubt. Her grandmother was still popular and had lots of friends. She had the kind of beauty that didn't fade. In addition to her smooth cocoa skin, and her thick white hair, which she kept in two braids twisted on top of her head, she had bright brown eyes and a beautiful smile that erased her years.

Greta was the opposite. She had few friends, especially in high school, and didn't want to go back and see them. "I'm happy with my life."

Her grandmother sent her a look, stripping away the false ring of her words.

"Most of it anyway," Greta clarified. "There's no one I want to see."

Her grandmother rested her hands in her lap. "Don't you want more?"

Yes. But what Greta wanted seemed out of reach. Her life revolved around her family. Greta's sister, Marlene, had kicked a nasty drug habit six months ago and was now trying to rebuild her life. Marlene had gotten a new job and her own apartment, and her fortune teller had told her (for a price) that her life was headed for love and riches.

Greta was glad her sister was happy, but wasn't pleased her sister was spending what little money she made on a fortune teller she saw as her lifeline. Greta distrusted anything non-scientific; Marlene, however, could be sold magic beans. She was easily manipulated. That was how she'd ended up with a drug habit at fifteen. Her first boyfriend in high school convinced her that using drugs would make her cool. Two years later she'd had a daughter with a man she'd known only a month, who'd said he loved her. No, Greta didn't trust her sister's judgment but in spite of this, she loved her and hoped that her life had finally turned around.

Her older sister had mirrored their mother, Rita's, life— many men and several rehabs later. Rita, like her mother Minnie, had managed to keep her good looks and could pick up a man whenever she felt in the mood, which was often. But she'd never been able to hold a job and now, at sixty, blamed ageism for her latest job disaster. Greta knew that her mother's recent job loss was due more to her mother's tardiness and attitude than her age. But her mother never took responsibility for anything. Which was why, for the past twenty-six years, Greta had been providing for the entire household.

Minnie had never gotten on with her only daughter Rita, and after a major shouting match, that left them both hoarse, her grandmother packed up her bags and moved in with her son who lived in South Carolina. It had been a big loss for Greta. Initially, she felt abandoned by the one person she depended on. Her grandmother couldn't fight for custody of Greta, because at the time Minnie wasn't a citizen and did not have permanent status (her husband had never gotten around to filing her papers, and by the time he disappeared, her visa had expired), and was afraid that Rita would disclose her status as an illegal immigrant. (Minnie later applied for and got her green card). So Minnie did what she could, sending her grand-daughter cards filled with money and calling once a month.

Greta had just turned eight when she discovered why her grandmother had been so angry with her mother. A kid at school, who was annoyed with Greta for being such a "smarty pants", had sniffed and said "Doesn't matter 'cause your Mom's a druggie!"

This explained many things about her mother's behavior—the mood swings, the mess, the men. Fortunately, her mother was clean now, but she was totally dependent on her.

After her grandmother left, a tiny war started between Greta and her mother. No matter where they lived, their tiny apartment would end up hosting a number of her mother's "friends".

By twelve, Greta decided to take over and set down the rules. Their apartment was to be a "woman only" household. If her mother wanted a man to move in, Greta would be gone. Her mother had laughed. "You're just a little girl and you think you can tell me what to do? You two need a father and I'm trying to get you one."

"I don't need a father," Greta shot back. "I don't want one. I don't like the men you get." Once, she'd been excited about having a 'father'. She was eight. Minnie was gone and she was eager to have a family like the ones she'd seen on TV. But she'd soon learned that all men weren't meant to be fathers. One guy always passed out stone drunk on the living room floor; another guy was sweet, but he always smelled like weed, and didn't work. By twelve she'd cast her dream of being a typical American family aside. Listening to some of the girls at school, she'd heard what stepdads and boyfriends could do and after seeing it happen up close (her mother's boyfriend pretended to lose his way and went into Marlene's room and assaulted her) Greta was determined she would be the head of the household.

Always resourceful, she'd taken in cleaning for other residents in the apartment building where they lived. She did housekeeping chores, washed, ironed and folded laundry for extra money. For those who couldn't pay, she accepted old clothing, used furniture and food in exchange. When Minnie had lived with them, Greta had always stayed close to her and had learned, at an early age, how to wash and iron clothes. She loved when Minnie told her stories of how she made a living washing clothes by hand for rich families, and how skilled she was at ironing.

Greta hadn't spent her time playing with local kids, instead she was always by Minnie's side, learning how to sort the colors, so that they wouldn't get ruined, and learning how to iron shirts and blouses. Minnie also took her shopping and taught her how to cook delicious meals, using a variety of seasonings and spices to enhance the flavor. Marlene never showed an interest in being domestic, and her mother was too busy pleasing whichever man she was with, so most of the responsibility had fallen to Greta.

She never complained, she cherished her time alone with Minnie, and loved being "special". Once Minnie was no longer around, and she could see that both her mother and sister were unstable, Greta knew the role she had to play. She'd keep them safe. But her mother wouldn't agree to her rules and the men kept coming, until one fateful day when Greta was forced to take control. Her mother's latest boyfriend had lasted the longest (eight months to be exact) and Greta didn't mind him too much, because he helped pay the rent, instead of giving the money to her mother to blow on drugs. Greta didn't mind having him stay around, until that day.

She was sharing a room with Marlene, who was seventeen at the time, and her nine month old niece, Brianna. She'd come home from school and found her mother's boyfriend in their bedroom. He was on their bed, straddled on top of her sister with his pants and underwear around his ankles.

Brianna was in her cot and Marlene was passed out on the bed. The man was too busy looking at Marlene to notice Greta standing frozen in the doorway. Greta took in everything, especially the look on his face. She instantly knew it wasn't love. She couldn't quite categorize it, all she knew was that his look scared her and she needed to do something fast. Greta raced to the kitchen, grabbed a butcher knife then returned to the bedroom and shouted. "Get out!"

The man spun around and swore. "I was just jerking off, I wasn't going to do anything."

"Get out!" Greta approached him with the knife held out.

Her niece started to cry. Her sister didn't move.

The man scrambled off the bed and pulled up his pants. "Where's Rita?"

Greta gripped the knife tighter, her fear growing. He wasn't afraid. She wanted him to be, but he looked calm, almost smug. He wasn't intimidated by the knife or her. She was just a kid and he wasn't going to leave. She darted to the bed and pretended to search for something under the mattress.

"What you doing?"

"Looking for my mother's gun."

The man jumped over the bed and yanked her up by the collar of her shirt. "You don't need that. Nothing happened."

"Get out!"

He covered her mouth, pressing her body tight against his. His voice was soft. "No one needs to know about this." He held her in a way so that she couldn't bite him. "It's going to be okay. I'll take care of all of you." His free hand slid down her chest, over her budding breasts. "Hmm, you're starting to fill out. You're a young woman now."

Bile rose up in Greta's throat, but she waited for him to lose his hold.

"Okay now?"

She nodded.

"Good." He released her and the moment he did she spun around and sunk the knife blade into his shoulder. He screamed.

Rita came into the room holding her head. "What's the screaming for?"

"The bitch stabbed me," the man said, gripping his shoulder while blood seeped through his fingers.

"He was in here with his pants down," Greta said.

"Marlene asked me to. You've seen how she's been looking at me."

At that moment Greta saw her mother looking at her daughter as a rival, instead of a victim. And Greta knew the man was trying to ruin her family with lies. She lunged at him again, but her mother grabbed her. Rita slapped her hard across the face and shoved her against the wall. "Watch yourself girl."

"I can't believe she stabbed me."

"Get in the car," Rita told him. "I know someone who can help you." Her mother glared at her daughter. "We'll talk when I get back." She left.

Greta grabbed her crying niece, rocking her to calm her. "Don't worry, he won't come back. You'll be safe now." She looked at her sister, still passed out, wishing she would act like the older sister and take care of them. She hated being small. Thankfully, neither her niece nor her sister remembered what happened. But Greta knew she wouldn't always be around to rescue them. Marlene was very pretty, and available, and men often took advantage of her. She had learned, at an early age, to use her looks to get what she wanted, just like their mother.

Hours later Rita returned, without the man. Greta sat in the kitchen feeding Brianna. Her mother slammed her purse on the table. "You stupid bitch. You just got rid of our meal ticket."

"I'll take care of us."

"He was just having fun. Your sister's pretty; jerking off is what men do. Besides, it's not like he's her father."

"It's not right."

"You're going to regret this."

But she didn't. When she turned sixteen, Greta managed to get an after school and week-end job that supported them all. Her mother had to keep her men and drug dealers outside the house. Her mother, and unfortunately her sister, continued using, and at times they would come home wasted, but there wasn't much Greta could do. During these difficult times, school had been her sanctuary.

And, since that incident with Marlene and the man on top of her, men hadn't played a part in her life. Not that she didn't want them to. But she didn't have the time, and the few guys she was attracted to didn't show any interest in her. So it hadn't been hard for her to stay single. It was expected.

At least ten years ago, she'd been able to move her family out of the city and into the fresh air of suburbia. Rita found the suburbs boring, but stayed; her niece, Brianna, thrived. But when Marlene got clean, she and Brianna abruptly up and left. It hurt Greta that Brianna chose to live with Marlene, instead of her.

Since the day Marlene had brought Brianna home from the hospital, Greta had played the role of mother. She was the one who fed her when she woke up in the middle of the night; she was the one who made sure there was money to pay for the medicine she needed when she had gotten bronchitis; Greta was the one who had been there when Brianna had taken her first steps, and who made sure the 'tooth-fairy' left a dollar bill for every tooth she place under her pillow. It was Greta, not Marlene who had gone with her on the first day of school and who had arranged for her to go with a neighbor and her children, when walking to and from school. By the time they moved out, Minnie had moved back to the area and was now living in the senior community. This had been a comfort. "She knows her mother needs her," she'd told Greta.

"And I don't?"

"No, you need your own life."

And that was the same argument her grandmother used to convince her to go to the reunion.

"You need to do something for yourself. You're at a critical stage in your life Greta."

"The biological clock ticking and all that?" Greta said with a laugh.

"No, it's much more than that. Now is the time for you to reflect on what you want your future to look like."

"By going back to my past?"

"Yes, you are ready."

"Ready for what?"

"Your life to begin."

"It already has."

Minnie shook her head, looking a little sad. "Not fully. You've put your personal life on hold to take care of your family and if you're not careful, you'll be doing that for the rest of your life."

"No, I won't. Marlene is clean now and Brianna is doing great at her part time job."

"And your mother?"

"Hasn't gotten into trouble for the past year." Which was saying a lot.

"You have to go to the reunion. Just to get out of your rut. Your destiny could be there. I had a dream about that."

"I don't believe in destiny."

"How about love?"

"Maybe."

"Then what about that. What if a man from your past is your true love?"

"You're just a romantic."

"Is there anyone you can remember with fondness?"

"From high school?"

"Yes."

Greta couldn't think of anyone she'd want to see again. All she could remember were the typical uncreative taunts—Four Eyes, geek, ugly. And there were the more creative ones, like coconut or Oreo (brown on the outside but white on the inside), loser, weirdo. She'd been a smart kid in a school, where beauty and athletics ruled. Even the teachers thought her ambition to become a prominent scientist strange. No one expected much from the students. They were just kids who attended a poor DC public school with a low graduation rate, and no expectations of aspiration. But, in spite of the peeling paint, broken desks, used text books, and a disinterested teaching staff, school had still been a better place than home. It was a place where Greta was able to imagine her life being something more. She thought for a moment. She couldn't think of any boy from the past who she'd want to see.

Then she stopped, as a face began to form in her mind. No, she had been wrong. There had been, still was, one person who lingered in her mind nearly twenty years later. Drake Henson. Could he be the one her grandmother was referring to? Could she really dare to dream that big?

"You've thought of someone?" her grandmother said with a knowing smile.

Oh yes. Greta made a noncommittal sound.

"It may or may not be him. Keep your heart open. I want you to be happy."

Happiness with a man seemed like a foreign concept. Greta brushed the thought of Drake aside. "But I am—"

"Greta." Her grandmother grabbed her hand and gave her a fierce look. "You can lie to yourself, but not to me. Remember what I said. Keep your heart open. All men aren't the beasts you've made them out to be."

Greta laughed. "I don't think that."

"But you don't trust them."

No, she didn't trust them. But she also didn't need them. She had male colleagues. She was one of the few females in her department. They never looked at her with any personal interest and that was fine with her. "They never pay attention to me anyway," she said. But Drake had once. He'd been so kind. She remembered the deep island lilt he had when he spoke. In school, he always seemed preoccupied, almost other-worldly. She wondered what thoughts he had. His kindness didn't seem real. She'd never seen a young man so nice before. He never belittled her. Once, when the teacher had announced the three top grades for an exam, she'd gotten the highest score.

While other kids had sneered, he'd given her a brief pat on the back and said "Good job". It had been an absent, casual gesture, lacking any true intimacy, but it had been a crumb of kindness to a girl who'd been starving for affection. Unfortunately, it made her desperate for more. So desperate she'd made herself available to his younger brother, Eric, just to get his attention. At the time, Eric was much smaller than his older brother, he wore glasses like her, and was rather quiet. Her scheme hadn't worked. She'd given his brother his 'first time', and hers, and Drake still didn't know she existed.

It had been a new low for her. And it had scared her. She remembered that Minnie had come for a short visit, at that time, and had noticed a change in her.

"What's going on wid you girl?" she asked as Greta helped her put away her clothes. She sat on the bed, watching her.

"Nothing." Greta opened a drawer and placed a top inside. She'd given her grandmother the room she shared with Brianna and Marlene. They would room with Rita while Greta would sleep on the couch. "I hope there's enough room here for everything you brought."

Minnie's keen gaze sharpened. "Someting different." Greta knew when her grandmother spoke patois, it was an indication that she was either very relaxed or serious, and she didn't sound relaxed.

Greta pulled out another top and kept her voice neutral. "What do you mean?"

"I'm too ole for games. I know when a girl becomes a woman. Look at mi."

Greta swallowed then turned.

"What you up to?"

Greta shrugged then saw her grandmother frown and knew she could see right through her and the thought terrified her. Her grandmother's opinion meant everything and she didn't want to disappoint her. She didn't want to do or say anything that would send her away. "I have my period, Minnie. That's all. There's nothing else going on."

"Why you wearing your hair like dat?"

Greta touched her new hairstyle with trembling fingers, feeling bare and vulnerable. Since sleeping with Eric hadn't made a difference, she had been trying to fix herself up and change her image to get Drake to notice and like her. She desperately wanted him to see her, but he hadn't noticed a thing. Unfortunately, her grandmother had. "I just wanted to try something different. Is that a crime?"

Minnie's frown increased. "Don't try fi talk fast wid me Greta. That's not you. Who you want to be? Your mother or yourself?"

She never answered her grandmother's question, but that very day, she'd gone back to pulling her hair back in a ponytail, and wearing her comfortable clothes, instead of wearing close fitting sweaters to show off her figure. She'd borrowed some of Marlene's clothes, without her knowledge of course, but she had taken them off as soon as she got home because they made her feel so awkward she'd kept her jacket on all day.

After her grandmother's visit, the thought that she could be just as much a user as her mother and sister had terrified her. She realized that she'd been too eager for male attention, just like them, but seeing where that kind of neediness could lead, she'd gotten over it fast. Greta promised herself that she would never use someone or be used. She'd be self reliant. After the fiasco with Eric, Greta focused on graduating from high school, going to college, and getting out of the city. Men were not for her. She wasn't good for them and they weren't good for her. She vowed she'd never let herself become that susceptible again.

Greta earned her undergraduate and master's degree, then got an excellent job and bought her own house. Compared to most of her classmates, she knew she was a success. Several years ago she had been featured in a major national magazine and listed as one of a few black scientists making a name for herself in environmental issues. She had achieved most of what she'd dreamed of, except a family of her own.

Could Drake be part of her future? She didn't believe in true love, it only belonged in fairy tales. She hadn't seen it in her life. She'd seen it in movies and read it in books and listened to it in love songs, but that was all. She hadn't, and didn't see true love being part of her life. But maybe, just maybe she'd see Drake again and ...

"I'll go" Greta said.

Minnie beamed. "Good. Go and have fun."

Fun. Greta thought back to her grandmother's words as she looked at a crude drawing on the bathroom stall. She laughed bitterly. She wasn't having fun. She shouldn't' have come at all. She'd placed too much hope on this night. She should have known better.

GRETA HAD DECIDED to go straight to the reunion after work. Before leaving her office building, she'd gone into the bathroom and changed. She'd selected to wear the only decent outfit she had in her closet along with a pair of leather two-inch heels she had bought for the occasion. Getting dressed up wasn't something she was comfortable doing. At work, since she spent a lot of time working in the lab, she always wore a white lab coat. And, for day to day wear, she opted for comfortable, rather than stylish, shoes. She let her hair out and spent time curling her shoulder length hair with a curling iron, unable to tame a shiver of excitement. Going to the reunion would be like going to the prom she never went to. Part of her wished she had a date or a friend to go with her to the event, but she was used to being alone, so she quickly dismissed the idea.

Greta entered the school, not surprised that the committee hadn't been able to rent a classy hall or glamorous ballroom for the event. She picked up her name tag, which was arranged alphabetically on a table off to the side, then turned and walked down the hallway and entered the cafeteria. The first thing she saw were gold and black streamers and balloons (their school colors) and several of the organizers rushing around making last minute preparations. She didn't know any of them, so she walked over to the side and leaned against a wall. She'd come too early. She'd never learned to be fashionably late nor did she know how to make an entrance. No one noticed her. Greta looked at her badge and saw they'd spelled her name wrong. GERTA. Oh well. It didn't matter, she looked forward to the evening and possibly seeing Drake again. She hoped he'd come. But as the evening progressed her hopes dwindled and then she saw him.

CHAPTER TWO

He was just as beautiful as she'd remembered him. Grayer than she'd expected, but that didn't take away from his gorgeous amber eyes, smooth brown skin, and impressive build. She rushed over to him and squinted at his badge, pretending she was trying to remember who he was, although she didn't need to. "I don't believe it. Drake Henson?"

He sent her a wary look. "Yes."

She remembered that most about him. He was cautious with strangers. "You haven't changed a bit," she continued wishing she could get her racing heart under control. "You still look like you'd rather be somewhere else."

"Bad habit of mine."

"What's your name?" a female voice asked.

Greta paused. She hadn't noticed the woman standing beside Drake, although she should have. She was an attractive, full figured woman, with a kind smile. Greta tugged on her badge a little sheepish for being so single focused. She should have guessed he would have brought someone, she just assumed since he'd been a loner in high school that hadn't changed. "They misspelled my name. I'm Greta Rodgers. It's all right if you don't remember me."

"I remember you," Drake said in a warm voice that washed over her like a fresh spring breeze. He still had the voice she remembered so well, and it still made her skin tingle. "Physics whiz who played the clarinet."

He really remembered her? "Yep, that was me. I'm a physicist now. If the rumors are true, you're a successful restaurateur. Not too bad for our class." Of course she hadn't heard any rumors, she'd looked him up online.

"I didn't do it alone. Cassie's been my rock."

Her heart fell. "Cassie?"

Drake affectionately touched the woman beside him. "Yes, my wife. She helps me with the recipes, design, and a number of other projects and she also has her own job as a speaker. If you're still single, and need a little confidence booster, you should think about attending one of Cassie's seminars. They're amazing. That's how we first met. Actually—" He stopped when his wife nudged him.

"Nice to meet you," Greta said, fighting to keep her voice light, although she felt like falling through the floor.

Cassie smiled with sympathy. "Likewise."

Cassie's sympathy made her feel worse. She didn't want to be pitied. Greta forced a grin. "Figures you'd be married. I'd hoped with all the divorces you'd be one of them." Greta felt heat steal into her cheeks, she didn't mean to sound that brazen. She needed to escape. "It was nice to see you again."

Drake frowned. "You don't have to leave. I could get you two ladies a drink and—"

"No, thanks," Greta said quickly. "I'd better go see who else I can recognize." She quickly turned and made her way over to the punch bowl, wishing it was a large brandy or whisky. Couldn't they even afford any liquor?

He was married. Not just married. *Happily* married. Greta felt like someone had ripped her heart out and squeezed the life out of it. What was worse was seeing the sympathy and compassion in his wife's eyes. Greta knew his wife could see that she still had feelings for Drake. How pathetic, to carry a crush for so long. Why couldn't he have been less attractive, or at least, less kind? He'd remembered her. It would have been easier if he hadn't. Greta watched Drake seek out Brenda Timmons, she had been their Prom Queen. No surprise. Men always did. No one sought her out. That was how it always had been and likely always would be. Why had she let her grandmother—a romantic—convince her that life could be otherwise?

Greta left the cafeteria and hid in the bathroom, where she'd been for the past ten minutes. She'd been such a fool to come. There was no one there remotely interested in her. A man from her past? What garbage. She'd set herself up. She was usually more practical. Harboring a crush for this long was juvenile. Drake could still make her knees weak and he was *still* blind to her feelings. She was pathetic. Greta knew she couldn't hide in the bathroom forever. She was about to open the door to the stall when she heard the bathroom door open.

"I know. She looked pathetic," a woman said. "Oh, and did you see Greta?"

Greta took a step forward to listen.

"Who could miss her in that retro dress?" her companion replied.

"She probably dragged it kicking and screaming from the 80's." They laughed uproariously.

"Heard she's a scientist or something."

"She'd have to have brains looking like that."

"And her tongue's still dragging on the floor for Drake." *They saw it too?!*

"I know. You'd think she'd know better. He's way out of her league."

"Can't blame her, lots of girls had crushes."

"My god, did you see his wife?"

The other woman laughed. "A real porker."

"At least she's pretty and I hear he owns a restaurant or something. He'd need a woman who likes to eat."

"That's probably the only way he can feed her."

Both women laughed.

Greta gripped her hands. It was high school all over again. No, it was worse. In high school, at least she had her dreams to sustain her. Now, she would soon reach forty without having achieved half of the things she had thought she would. Like winning a Nobel Peace Prize or curing a major disease. Instead, she'd spent most of her life supporting her mother, sister and niece. They were right, she wasn't a great dresser, but who cares? She didn't mind them making fun of her, she was used to it, but making fun of Drake's wife, Cassie, bothered her.

Greta walked out of the stall and the two women abruptly stopped laughing. She tried not to stare. She recognized them. The only reason she knew their names was because they had been the popular kids, and also among her tormentors. Chantal Gilmore, a former member of the dance team was a gaunt looking woman, wearing long false eye lashes, pink lipstick and a blonde wig or weave, Greta couldn't tell which. Her companion, Lanesha Charles, was on the chubby side.

She was wearing a pair of enormous gold earrings and sported three party rings on each hand, and evidently thought that wearing a tight, black, lycra dress would make her appear slimmer. Unfortunately, the dress only emphasized her rolls. Greta knew they felt sorry for her, but she felt sorry for them. They were still stuck in the role of looking down on others in order to feel important. As she had done in the past Greta decided to ignore their remarks and be as pleasant as possible.

"Hi Lanesha," Greta said in a bright voice. "How many kids do you have?" she asked, knowing it was a safe topic of conversation.

"Three. You?"

"None, no surprise there, right?" She turned to Chantal. "Did you ever get into modeling?"

"I'm in retail now."

Greta held back a grin, briefly imagining Chantal working at a discount store folding shirts. "Great," Greta said with faint praise. "Well, bye." She dried her hands then left. She heard the two women burst into laughter.

It was best to just leave. There was no reason to stay. Greta grabbed her coat, walked out to the parking lot and got in her car and drove several blocks feeling her pent up energy begin to ebb. She had escaped. It was over and she'd never go back. She was turning down a street when she saw a tall man standing looking at his car's flat tire. He was in a bad place for a flat and he definitely had the wrong car—a shiny gold BMW. In that neighborhood it was like leaving fresh meat in front of a pack of wolves. He'd probably gotten lost, or tried to find a short cut to another part of the city. Hopefully he had a spare.

Greta pulled her car to the side and parked. It wasn't safe for him to be by himself until he got his car back in order. She crossed the street and walked over to him. He appeared bigger the closer she got to him. *He may be lost, but a thief would be taking a risk to attack him.*

"I'll find a pair of eyes for you while you change the tire," she said.

The man spun around. "A pair of eyes?"

Greta paused. He was younger than she'd expected, probably late thirties to early forties although the darkness didn't let her get a good look at him. "Yes, you need a pair, and fast, or you won't last a minute out here."

"I'll last," he said in a grim tone.

"That's some hot property. Did you get lost or something?"

"Or. Something."

Clearly he wasn't in the mood to be sociable, but that didn't bother her. Greta was used to surly male behavior. "Just give me a minute."

The man went to his trunk. "You could look out for me."

She laughed. "I don't have that kind of power." She glanced around then saw a male figure across the street. He had a body like a slinky—wiry and flexible—with a bouncy walk, as if he was always ready to run. High Flyer. She knew him. She was in luck. "Don't move. I'll be right back." Greta darted across the street.

Rita had made her very aware of the different dealers in the city. High Flyer was a man she'd become acquainted with, through a friend of her mother's. He'd gotten his nickname because he was a drug dealer to the upper crust of DC society. He never had to go to them, they came to him. She knew that many of his associates lived in the area, although few knew where he lived. He had a code, which she respected, and which made him a man with a lot of reach and connections. She walked up to him. "I need a favor."

High Flyer stared at her surprised then shook his head. "Sweetness, you know I don't work this side. I don't need no trouble."

"I know, but—"

"However, lead the way, Sweetness, I'll make an exception. How high you wanna fly?"

"I don't want that."

"What's up then?"

"I need eyes on a car. I'll make it worth your while."

"What kind of wheels we talking 'bout?"

Greta nodded to the BMW.

High Flyer gave a low whistle. "That's gonna cost you."

"I know." Greta handed him a fifty dollar bill.

"That gets you ten." He pulled out his cell phone and started to dial.

"Ten?"

"It shouldn't take more than ten minutes," he said, looking at the well dressed man lift a spare tire and jack out of the trunk of his car.

"But—"

He turned away and spoke into his phone. "Yea, I got a watch job. Yea, you see it too? I know. But don't touch and make sure no one else does. Good." He put his cell phone away then turned to Greta. "Done."

"Thanks."

"I've got some info for you. It's 'bout Rita."

Greta felt her gut clench, but kept her voice calm. "What about her?"

"The guy she's seeing is bad news."

"They always are."

"I mean this one's real bad news. She needs to cut him loose. I'm not one to tell people what to do, but that's how I see it. He's connected to a lot of crap, and he's in deep. And I'm not talking shovel deep, Sweetness. I'm talking forklift."

Greta nodded, taking his information to heart. A warning,

coming from a drug dealer who also had a prostitution ring on the side, meant a lot. "Thanks."

"No problem." He left.

Greta returned to the man who was already changing his tire. "You better work fast."

"Trust me, I'm going as fast as I can." He removed the flat tire and replaced it with the spare.

He moved with a confidence that reminded her of someone, but Greta couldn't imagine who. She shook her head. She was just trying to place everybody because of the reunion, he was a stranger and it was best to leave him alone.

"So where are you headed?" she asked, just in case he needed directions.

"Home."

"If you have a map I can—"

"I can find my way home."

Yes, he clearly wanted to be left alone and she would oblige him. Greta turned.

"Thanks," he grumbled.

"You're welcome." She walked back to her car and was about to pull out her keys when she felt something hard strike the back of her head. She stumbled forward then spun around and whacked her assailant with her purse, stunning him. But when she looked at his eyes she realized she'd made an error. His pupils were dilated. He was high on something and now he was both enraged and fearless. Unlike a regular thief, she knew he wouldn't disappear into the darkness for another prey. He would stay and fight and she was no match for him.

The man grabbed for her throat and she clawed at his hands. Greta thought about her grandmother having to bury her and got the strength to fight back, but she started to see dots as oxygen left her. Then she was slammed to the ground—

his hands no longer around her neck. She glanced over to the side and saw two blurry figures fighting on the ground. She scrambled and grabbed for her glasses, which had been knocked off her face. For a moment she couldn't decipher the two figures as they rolled in the darkness. But in an instant, she saw one of them gain dominance. She noticed the cut of his jacket, and knew he was the owner of the BMW. But this was no ordinary businessman. He had the moves of a street fighter — a raw lethal energy—and the mugger was no match. But even with her glasses on the two figures suddenly became blurry and the world began to spin.

"Sweetness, you gotta get up."

"High Flyer?" she said, her tongue feeling heavy in her mouth.

"Come on you gotta stay awake."

Greta tried but she couldn't get her mouth to move anymore, then darkness descended.

CHAPTER THREE

*I*n seconds it was over. Vance Minton saddled the thief who was scrambling to escape, clawing the ground like a wild animal.

"Call the police," he said to the man kneeling beside the woman who had helped him.

"They won't come, man. You might as well knock him out or let him go."

"Let him go?" Vance turned and looked at the man, who was still struggling. He punched him hard and the man went limp. Vance stood flexing his hand. "I'll call then."

"He's not worth your time, man."

"He tried to kill her."

"He tried to steal her purse for easy drug money, there's a difference."

"He's dangerous."

"He didn't have a gun. Look at him, he probably just started to shave."

"I don't care how old he is. He's a menace."

"Misguided."

Vance folded his arms. "Are you his attorney or something?"

The other man frowned. "She's hurt bad, man."

Vance rushed over to the woman on the ground and swore. The mugger had done more damage than he'd thought. What was worse was that he knew who she was, although he'd pretended not to. Anger blinded him. He spun around and glared at the fallen man. "I'm going to kill him."

The other man leaped up in front of him and grabbed his arm. "Forget him. I'll take care of business. Get her to a hospital. The police won't come here and neither will the ambulance. At least not in time. We're all she got."

Vance knew the guy was right. It wasn't a section of DC that the police liked going to. They might come eventually, but it was a risk. He lifted the unconscious Greta up and put her in the back of his car. "Follow me in her car. I don't want to leave it here."

"It'll cost."

"I know. Charge me when we get there."

She smelled leather. Greta slowly opened her eyes, trying to get a grasp of her surroundings. She was moving, but she wasn't in her car. She glanced up and saw a man driving. Why was he driving her car? No, that was wrong. Her car didn't have leather seats. What was she doing in his car? She remembered a fight and then nothing.

"What's going on?" she asked, her voice sounding like sandpaper.

"If you feel sick there's a plastic bag in the back near your head."

"I don't understand."

"I'm taking you to the hospital. I didn't want to wait for the ambulance."

"I don't need an ambulance."

Greta noticed his jaw twitch. "You got hit pretty hard."

"But —"

"You need to be checked out. You could have a concussion. It's not smart to street fight with a guy high on something."

"I didn't know that." She lay her head down, she felt a little woozy.

"You could tell by his MO. You were in an open space, he could easily be seen, and there weren't many escape routes. Why didn't you just give him your purse?"

"He hit me on the head. I was defending myself."

"Next time just give him what he wants."

Greta felt herself getting angry then noticed how the man's hands gripped the steering wheel. Was he tense because of her? Then she understood him trying to bait her. He was trying to keep her focused on something else, besides her injuries.

"I'll be okay," she said. "Wait. Where's my car?"

"Behind us."

She slowly sat up and turned. "High Flyer is driving my car? It's going to be expensive." She sighed, resigned. "Better than having it stripped, I suppose." She turned to him. "I don't need the hospital."

"This is not a discussion." Before she could argue he said, "What's your name?"

"Greta Rodgers."

She saw his shoulders tense. "What's your middle name?"

"Why?"

He shook his head. "Because I can't call you Greta."

"Why not?"

"It's just wrong for you. A black girl from a southeast DC high school with a Swedish name. What was your mother thinking?"

Strange? How did he know she was from a southeast DC high school? Maybe because he'd seen her talking to High Flyer and assumed she grew up in the area, in which case he'd be right. "My mother didn't name me. My grandmother did. She was also the one who took me home from the hospital." She added softly. "She loved old movies and her favorite actress was Greta Garbo."

"That's a nice story. Now what's your middle name?"

"I don't have one."

"I'll call you Reta."

"No."

"Why, not?"

"That's too close to my mother's name. Rita."

"Didn't you ever want to change your name? Didn't kids tease you at school."

"My name was only one reason."

"Hmm...fine I'll call you Tera."

They made it to the hospital in less than fifteen minutes and Vance drove Greta to the emergency room entrance. It wasn't a busy night, so Greta got seen quickly. She wondered if her rescuer would still be there when she was released.

"WHAT ON EARTH were you doing in that part of town?" Sylvie screeched on the other end of the line. "Do you have a death wish?"

Vance paced outside the hospital regretting calling his girlfriend. It was not a fun night. First a flat tire, then he was out three hundred bucks because of a guy with a name that reminded him of air travel. "I only called because I didn't want you to wait up for me."

"Your mother's here."

"Why?"

"She dropped by to visit and to remind you about tomorrow."

Vance knew his mother had stopped by to remind him about a luncheon she wanted him to attend. "I won't forget."

"She wanted to make sure."

"Just don't tell her about this."

"She already knows," a new, but familiar voice on the other line said. "Sylvie, let us talk."

Vance softly swore, he should have guessed his mother would be waiting on the line. His girlfriend was trying to be as close to his mother as possible. It was understandable, since they were expected to get married. He'd been seeing Sylvie for four years and he knew the writing was on the wall.

"What have you been up to?" his mother asked once Sylvie had hung up. Her words were more an accusation than a question.

"It's nothing."

"You've been acting strange lately, leaving work and not telling anyone where you were going."

The whirl of an ambulance filled the air. Vance wanted to go back inside before Greta was released. "I have to go."

"Where are you now?"

"At the hospital."

"Which hospital? Are you hurt?"

Vance looked down at his hand and flexed it, vaguely

wishing he could have done more damage to the mugger. "Southeast General. No, I was just helping someone."

"A woman?"

"Yes, but—"

"I knew it," his mother said, sounding satisfied with herself. "You were trolling for hookers and one got sick on you, right?"

"Mom."

"And you thought you had to save her."

He sighed. His mother always thought the worst of him. "No, she's not a hooker. I don't go for that."

"Your Uncle did."

"I don't."

She gasped. "Oh God, is it drugs?"

"No."

"Then what were you doing in southeast?"

"There's more to southeast than drugs and hookers. You know that. We lived here for a few years, remember?"

"You know that's something I *never* want to remember," she said, her tone cold. Vance knew he'd hurt her, because that time of their lives had been a painful one. It had been due to one of his father's bad dealings and it had been one of the reasons he'd learned to fight. After leaving a top prep school to attend one in the inner city, Vance knew he and his brother would be prime targets, so he'd made sure that no one would. Or that if they did, they would have regrets.

"I simply made a wrong turn."

"Really?"

He rubbed the back of his neck, trying to ease his anger. "Why do you always think the worst of me?"

"Because I don't understand you. You have no business being in the city that I know of, let alone southeast ."

"You can relax. It was a simple error."

"You're lying to me and I plan to find out why."

Vance shrugged. She was right. He'd been lying, but he wouldn't explain unless he was forced to. He wouldn't tell her that he'd impulsively decided to attend his high school reunion. A high school he'd barely graduated from. He'd wanted to show his old classmates how far he'd come. To show them how he'd turned his life around. No one had expected much from him.

He hadn't expected much from himself. He'd been a top basketball player in school and also made it his hobby to charm as many young women as he could. He and his friends made a game of going out with virgins and 'popping their cherry'. He'd been arrogant, cocky, and at times, heartless—until he'd been forced to change, but he wouldn't think about that now.

No, he didn't want to tell his mother about going to his class reunion or that he'd bumped into the last person he'd expected to see—Greta Rodgers, one of the girls he'd tormented. She didn't recognize him. That was a good thing. She hadn't liked him much and in truth, he hadn't liked her. She'd been so full of herself and he felt she looked down on him. A little nobody like her, looked at him as if he were a weasel. It had irked him, so he'd made her life miserable.

He hadn't recognized her at first. He'd just thought it funny for a young woman wearing an outdated, sheer, green ruffled dress and a pair of big glasses, offering him assistance. It was her smile that did it. She'd smiled at him and then helped him get some 'eyes' for protection. She'd been that way in school, too. Always willing to help others, despite the fact she was a social outcast. He'd tried to be brusque so she'd get annoyed and leave, but she didn't. Then he'd half expected her to recognize him, but she hadn't done that either.

She fascinated him. She wasn't what he expected. He

liked her boldness. How she looked him squarely in the eye. She both terrified and excited him. No woman met him eye to eye that way. Like a lioness to a lion. A recognition of equals. Yes, that was it. She was his equal and didn't mind expressing it, even though now he had a better car than she did, finer clothes and even better looks. And that was what tore at him, seeing her lying helpless on the ground just because she'd stopped to help him.

"Van, are you listening?"

"No. Gotta go, talk to you later." He turned off his phone and put it away, then headed back inside. At first he'd wanted to get rid of Greta but now she was the only person he wanted to be with. He had to make sure she was alright.

AFTER ENDURING a series of tests and five stitches later, Greta was bruised but she would be okay. She was released and sent home with some pain medication.

"Your friend is in the waiting room," the discharge nurse told her as she helped her get dressed.

"Friend?"

"Yes, the man who brought you."

High Flyer had waited for her? That was out of character for him, he must have been paid well. Greta walked to the waiting room then stopped when she saw the stranger. He saw her and tossed his magazine aside and walked towards her. The bright lights of the hospital allowed her to have a clearer view of him. He was as tall as she remembered but he was a dark figure of a man—big and powerful. He looked like he'd brought the city streets with him. He was handsome with dark intense brown eyes. And he seemed oddly familiar.

"How are you feeling?" he asked.

Greta smiled. "Better than I look."

"Let me take you home." He held up his hand. "It's not a request. I'll take you in your car."

"But what about your car? How will you get home?"

"I'll take a taxi back here and pick it up then."

"But that's a lot of effort."

He flashed a quick grin. "Stop worrying about me. That's what got you into this mess."

"Getting mugged wasn't your fault."

"If you hadn't stopped to help me you'd be home safe right now."

"Then it could have been you."

"I would have preferred it."

"You don't mean that."

He gently took her arm. "Yes, I do. Now come on."

"But—"

"I told you not to worry about me. I'll be fine."

Greta bit her lip. She was glad for the help, so she wouldn't argue. "I don't even know your name."

He hesitated. "Vance Minton."

CHAPTER FOUR

e was going to say no. They were minutes from her house and Greta knew that if she asked him in for coffee, he was going to say no, but that didn't stop her from wanting to ask him. She didn't want the night to end, or her time with him to end. But she knew he would say no. He'd say that he was busy or that he had a wife waiting for him, or something. She quickly glanced at his left hand. He wasn't wearing a wedding ring. She figured he'd say he'd prefer to wait in the car until the taxi came. It was a shame, because she really liked him. He was easy to be with. He didn't question how she knew High Flyer, he had stayed with her at the hospital and instead of putting her in a taxi or just walking her to her car, he'd driven her home.

Vance Minton. She liked his name. And, like his face, there was something familiar about it, but she couldn't place it or him. She'd never see him again and he didn't seem to know her, so she might as well forget it. Greta saw her house come into view and sighed. Time to say goodbye. He pulled up into the driveway and parked.

Greta unlatched her seatbelt and opened the door. "Would you like to come in for coffee?"

"Sure."

She got out of the car. "Of course I understand. It's been a long evening...wait what?" She turned to stare at him over the hood of her car.

He closed the car door. "I said sure."

"Really?"

He flashed one of his quick grins. "Yes."

"Oh good." *He'd said yes. He had actually said yes.* Greta felt like skipping, but she had to play it cool. She had to play it as if she'd invited men for coffee all the time, even though this was the first time in her life. She didn't see her mother's car in the driveway, so that was a reprieve. Greta stepped inside her house pleased that it was clean. Her mother must have been out most of the day. They passed through the living room. He pointed to her music stand and clarinet case.

"You still play the clarinet?" he asked surprised.

"Yes, I play in an orchestra. It's not professional, it's just for fun." She stared at him. "How did you know I played the clarinet?"

He blinked. "It's just that most people who learn an instru-ment start as a child and then stop as an adult. I just assumed you'd started early."

"You're right. Very observant."

"Hmm."

"The kitchen is this way." He followed her but when they reached the kitchen he gently pushed her into a chair and said, "I'll make the coffee just tell me where things are."

"Okay." She sat and watched him. "So what do you do?"

"I'm a contractor."

"How exciting."

He looked at her unsure, as if he was trying to figure out if she was being serious. "You mean that?"

She nodded. "Building things and creating things have always fascinated me."

A faint smile touched his lips. "Me too."

Vance found what he needed and made the coffee then poured some into two mugs and set one in front of her. Greta smiled at him, wishing he would be more talkative. "Thanks Van."

"Vance," he corrected.

"Sorry," she said, surprised by his curt tone. "I thought since you call me Tera I could give you a nickname too."

Vance sat down in front of her. "I prefer you call me Vance."

She furrowed her brows. "Something about your name sounds familiar."

He gripped his mug with two hands. "It's a pretty common name."

"Not that common."

An awkward silence fell. So he didn't like nicknames and seemed uneasy. He was not as carefree as he'd been in the car. Had he said yes out of pity? Did he just need the coffee to keep him awake for a long drive home? Maybe she'd read too much into him saying yes—he'd said yes to the coffee, not her. She stood. "Well, let me call that taxi for you."

Vance looked at her stunned. "I just sat down and you want to get rid of me already?"

Greta slowly sat down, confused. "No, it's not that," she said stumbling over her words. "I just thought you may have somewhere else you need to be." She wasn't handling this well. What was she doing wrong? "Would you like something to eat?" Again, she expected him to say no, but instead he said, "That would be great."

"Do you mind leftovers? I have some curried lamb with garlic potatoes."

"Sounds delicious."

"But it may take a while to heat up."

"That's fine."

He seemed in no hurry to leave so she wouldn't force him. Greta went to the fridge and took out the dishes and gave them to Vance. He popped them in the microwave, while Greta excused herself to go change. She raced into her bedroom and found a pair of jeans and top she could wear. She looked at herself in the mirror. "Relax. He obviously wants to stay. Don't drive him away." She returned to the kitchen and found Vance eating with gusto. She tried not to stare. She had made more of the dish than she needed, because she planned on taking some with her for lunch, but at the rate he was eating, she knew there would be nothing left. He was a big man with evidently an appetite to match. "This is delicious," he said.

"Thank you."

"How did you learn to cook like this?"

"My grandmother."

"So, why were you all dressed up?"

She took a seat. "I just attended a high school reunion."

"Have fun?"

Greta sniffed and lifted a brow.

Vance grinned. "I'll take that as a 'No'."

"It was a silly, fanciful and dumb idea."

"Why dumb?"

"Dumb, for me anyway."

"Why?"

"Because, I remember the building with fondness and the people with pain."

"What does that mean?"

"My home life at the time was miserable so I loved going to school. In many ways, it was my escape, but the kids didn't like me. I didn't care too much then, but going back tonight brought back some of those hard times and memories. What about you?"

He paused, wary. "What about me?"

"How was high school for you?"

Vance stared down at his plate. "Let's talk about something else."

Greta pushed up her glasses, it was obviously a painful subject for him too. She could understand. Maybe he'd been small growing up and bullied or something. She reached out and touched his hand. "It's okay. You're not in high school anymore, thank goodness. You're a successful contractor and drive a great car. I bet you were just a late bloomer." And boy had he bloomed, Greta thought appreciating his handsome features.

"Hmm."

The more she talked the more he seemed to withdraw into himself. Greta wished she knew how to read him. He acted as if he didn't want to be there, yet made no attempt to leave. One moment he wanted to talk, then he closed up. She began to pull her hand away.

He grabbed it then kissed the back of it. "You're sweet."

Greta felt heat rush to her face, and her skin tingled from where his lips had touched her. Thankfully, his cell phone rang, giving her a reprieve from having to respond.

Vance looked at the number and scowled then put it back in his pocket. It stopped, then rang again.

"Maybe you should get that," she said.

"I'll get it later, it's just Sylvie."

"Sylvie?"

"Yes, my girlfriend."

He had a girlfriend. Of course. She'd struck out again. He'd only come for the coffee and the food. "Oh well," Greta said fighting to keep her voice light and cheery, two things she didn't feel. "She's probably worried about you." Greta stood. "Let me get that taxi." Her stomach grumbled.

Vance looked at her surprised. "You're hungry? Why didn't you say something instead of just watching me eat all your food?"

"You're a guest."

"A host can eat too. Go sit in the living room and I'll fix you something."

"But you—"

"I told you to stop worrying about me."

"Okay, but if you need any help—"

"Tera, shut up and go sit down." He softened his words with a smile and a wink.

Greta left the kitchen and sat in the living room, not knowing how to feel. She couldn't like him too much, because he had a girlfriend, but she could like him as a friend. She turned on the TV not caring what was on. Minutes later Vance came in carrying a tray of food. Greta couldn't believe what he had made. This guy was full of surprises. He had found several other items in her fridge and made a hearty stew. He had taken a can of tomato soup, mixed in the remaining curried lamb, added some diced potatoes, frozen vegetables, several seasonings and garnished with sliced onions.

"Wow! This looks great."

"Careful it's hot." He turned to the TV and noticed the

soccer match she'd been ignoring. "Is that Brazil against Argentina? Do you mind?" he asked, sliding into the seat next to her. He even smelled nice.

"No, I don't mind."

"My Dad and I used to love watching soccer together."

"Did you play in school?"

"No, we didn't have a team."

"That's true, it's not very popular here in the States as it is in other parts of the world. I'm surprised your father was interested. In the Caribbean it's a big deal. My grandmother likes to brag that she dated a footballer once."

"Yes, that's what my father calls soccer players too."

"Where's your father from?"

"Ghana."

"With the last name, Minton?"

"Hmm." His cell phone rang again and this time when he looked at the number he seemed like he was happy for the escape. "Excuse me." He left the room.

Greta didn't blame his girlfriend for being worried about him. She suppressed a sigh of longing and ate her food, trying not to think of Vance and what words he was saying to ease his girlfriend's fears. Would he be matter-of-fact, or tender? What side did he show to her that no one else saw?

"Anybody score?"

Greta looked up at him surprised by his quick return. She'd expected the phone call to last longer. "No," she said as he sat. "How is she?"

"Fine," he said with little interest. "I told her I'm okay. " He looked at her tray and furrowed his brows. "You haven't eaten much. Are you feeling okay?"

Greta was feeling much better now that he was back. "Sorry, I eat slowly sometimes."

He leaned back and rested an arm the length of the couch, as if he were settling for the evening. "As long as you're okay, I don't care." He turned his attention to the TV.

Greta ate and watched him. His profile was perfect. Or perhaps, she just saw it that way because she liked him so much. He was so considerate. She finished her food with reluctance. This was as close to dinner and a movie as she was ever going to get.

"Are you finished?" he asked.

Greta blinked again, amazed at how attuned he seemed to be to her. She'd thought all his attention had been focused on the match. "Yes, thanks."

He took the tray and headed for the kitchen. "I'm going to wash up. Call out the plays for me."

"The plays?"

"Yes, tell me what they're doing."

"I can wash up and you can—"

"Just tell me what you see."

Greta shrugged. "Number nine, Brazil is making his way down the middle and he just passed the ball to number thirty-four. Oh, wait, a turnover. Number twenty of Argentina steals the ball. They're scrambling to stop him, but he kicks it over their heads to number fourteen and then he tries to score but the goalie stops him."

"Ooo."

Greta relayed more plays and found herself enjoying it. Finally, Vance finished the dishes and joined her on the couch. They both shouted in unison when one of the teams made a tough score. "Goal!"

They hugged, and then settled into watching more of the game. She liked having him there. Strange, she'd never invited a man inside her home before. Never had a chance or a reason too. What made him feel so familiar to her? Everything felt so right. Greta felt her eyes getting heavy, her stomach was full, her body felt relaxed and all was well...

VANCE FELT Greta rest her head on his chest. He had his arm stretched out the length of the couch and made no move to pull away. She was exhausted and he didn't want to do anything to wake her. He felt responsible for and a little protective of her. He'd clammed up when she'd ask him about high school. He'd been king of the hill. It had been fun. Learning had been an extracurricular activity for him. Vance kept telling himself, he should be leaving, but came up with a reason to stay. She had a nice comfortable home and he'd meant it when he'd called her 'sweet'. Thank God she still didn't know who he was. He knew he had to leave, but he'd just stay a few minutes more. He couldn't remember the last time he'd enjoyed watching a soccer match. Soccer had been one of the few things that had brought him and his dad together. His dad had taught him a lot of moves, but then he learned that soccer wasn't as popular as basketball and when he made the varsity basketball team, although it hadn't been a favorite sport of his, he pretended it was, because what others thought of him back then really mattered. By the time he was ready to graduate from high school, the distance between him and his father had grown deep.

But being with Greta, enjoying the soccer game, just for a moment, took him back to happier times. To a time when he was just himself and didn't care about playing a role.

GRETA SLOWLY OPENED HER EYES, feeling as if someone was staring at her. She looked up and saw a blurry figure standing in front of her. She reached for her glasses, which sat on her lap. Funny, she didn't remember taking them off. She shoved them on then looked at her mother, who stood with her arms folded.

"So you can break the rules and I can't?"

"What are you talking about?" Greta rubbed her eyes and groaned. Her body felt as if it had been squashed by a bus.

"Him." Rita nodded to Vance. Greta turned realizing she had been resting her head on his chest. She also felt his arm around her shoulders. How had that happened? She sprang up. And what was he still doing there?

Her quick motion woke him. Vance opened his eyes and looked at her. "Are you feeling okay?"

"I'm fine."

"Good." He stretched, paused and looked around. Daylight flooded through the windows. "What time is it?"

"One thirty," Rita said.

Vance sat up, instantly awake. "In the afternoon?"

"Do you think it'd be this bright in the morning?"

"That has to be wrong."

"It's not wrong."

Vance glanced at his watch, then jumped up and swore. "She's going to skin me alive."

Rita sneered. "Your wife?"

"No, his girlfriend," Greta said.

"No, my mother," he said. "I was supposed to meet her for some function." He swore.

"Just tell her you were helping me."

"Helping you do what?" Rita asked.

"Nothing," Greta said in no mood to explain. "Let me call

you a cab. You can go freshen up in the bathroom down the hall. There's a package in the medicine cabinet for visitors." She didn't mention that the visitors were usually her mother's and that's why she always had a freezer bag with a travel size toothbrush, tooth paste, mouth wash, bar of soap, a washcloth and deodorant.

"Thanks." He left.

Greta placed a call for a taxi then headed into the kitchen to make some coffee.

Rita followed her. "He's gorgeous. Who is he?"

Greta waved her away. "Just a good Samaritan."

"What's up with your face? Did you two get in a fight or something?"

"Or something," Vance said in a cool dismissive way as he reached for a cup.

"The cab is on its way," Greta said, wishing her mother would leave so they could be alone.

"Good." He took a sip of his coffee, his eyes assessing Greta as if there was no one else in the room. "How's your head?"

"How's your lip?"

He flashed a crooked smile. "Sore."

"Me too. If your girlfriend or mother gives you too much grief, have them call me."

Vance took out his wallet and handed her a card. "Call me if you need anything else."

"Did you two meet at the reunion?" Rita asked, a little louder than necessary, jealous that she wasn't the center of attention.

"Yes," Greta said.

"No," Vance said.

Rita frowned. "You don't know?"

"It was *after* I left the reunion," Greta said.

Vance gestured to the door. "I'll wait for the taxi outside. You should go back and rest."

Her mother sniffed. "What for?"

"She was attacked last night."

"Really? Someone got the better of you? That's incredible. My Greta can take on the world." She squinted at him. "Why do you look familiar? What's your name?"

"Vance Minton." He left.

Greta grabbed her mother's arm before she could follow him. "Leave him alone."

Rita yanked her arm away. "I know I've seen that face before."

Greta wished the taxi would hurry up. Her mother was being more obnoxious than usual, probably because Vance was good looking. She wouldn't have bothered otherwise.

He probably got that a lot. Women throwing themselves at him. No wonder he was so eager to leave. Greta walked outside and found Vance resting against the wall. Something had shifted from last night, his profile seemed more stoic and distant. Was he regretting helping her? "It's chilly out here," she said seeing his jaw tense. "Do you need a sweater or something?"

He turned to her and his mouth softened into a smile. "I'm fine." He pinched her nose. "How am I going to get you to stop worrying about me?"

Never. Greta hugged herself, wishing she could hug him goodbye instead.

Rita came through the door and pointed at him. "Now I remember." She snapped her fingers. "I keep trying to think, because I never forget a pretty face, and then I thought basketball and you're name came to mind."

Vance stiffened. "Look don't—"

"'Van the Man'. Yes, that's who you are. That's what every-body called you because you were hot property. You were even written up in the papers a couple of times."

Greta stared at Vance stunned. For the second time in twenty-four hours, Greta wanted the floor to open up and disappear. All of the wonderful memories of that night came crashing down. She was staring at 'Van the Man'. One of the high school boys who'd made her life back then a living hell.

CHAPTER FIVE

"I go by Vance now," he said, his gaze not leaving Greta's face.

Rita just grinned. "Sure you do, honey."

Greta shook her head, feeling stupid as everything clicked into place. "You were there to attend the reunion. You were heading in the right direction, until you got a flat tire."

"Yes."

"Sorry you missed it." She turned and went to the door. What foolish feelings she'd felt didn't matter now. He was leaving soon and she'd never see him again. There would be no friendship between them; he'd just needed a place to crash. He had a fine, hot, girlfriend at home. She remembered he'd juggled a few while in high school. "Brenda was there, looking great as always and—"

"I don't feel like I missed anything." Vance took a step forward, but halted when Greta took a step back. "Listen, I don't regret—"

Greta could no longer hold his gaze and glanced out at the

street. "Taxis don't usually take this long." She turned to the house. "I'll give them another call."

"Tera—"

She spun around and blinked back tears, saddened that even the nickname he'd given her now felt like a mockery. "My name is Greta." She went inside and closed the door, wanting to slam it, but knowing that a petty action like that would only please Rita.

Greta went into her bedroom and sat on the bed. She was an idiot. How did her mother remember him and she didn't? 'Van the Man'. The hotshot basketball star. How could she have not recognized or remembered him? Back then he went by Van Lamine. She'd spent the evening with one of her worse tormentors. No, he didn't torment her directly, his friends did. He just stood by and watched with enjoyment. She wondered if he'd secretly been laughing at her the whole night, as she invited him in for coffee, then later when she held his hand and tried to comfort him about the terrible time, she imagined, he'd had in high school. What a laugh! She heard the taxi drive up and gripped her hands into fists. "Goodbye you bastard," she muttered. She'd let her grandmother's silly dream lead her astray, again. But now she was back to her senses.

Greta gathered herself and went into the kitchen to make herself something to eat. Her mother was finishing off a slice of toast, leaving a trail of crumbs on the counter.

"So you really didn't know who he was?" she asked, with a superior smirk.

Greta wiped the crumbs away with a wet dish towel, then reached up and took a box of cereal out of one of the cabinets. She poured the cereal into a bowl, ignoring the question. "Who are you seeing?"

"Why?"

"Because there's word on the street he's bad news."

"Word from who? People been talking trash in your ivory tower?"

Greta poured some milk on her cereal then grabbed a spoon and sat down. Her mother liked to make fun of her job, although it was the very thing that kept them fed and a roof over their head. "I heard it from somewhere."

"You think I'd take advice about men from a woman like you? You wouldn't know what to do with one if you had a chance. You don't know anything about men."

Little did her mother know, she'd learned a lot from Eric,

although she hadn't had the chance to use her knowledge on anyone else. Greta ate a spoonful of cereal then mumbled under her breath, "Looking at your record I don't think you do either."

Her mother lifted her hand, as if to strike her.

Greta met her gaze in a silent challenge. "Just try."

Rita lowered her hand. "I don't know why you like pissing me off."

"I'm just trying to help you."

"My private life is none of your business."

"I don't want you to get hurt."

"You're going to pretend to care about me now?"

Greta slammed her spoon down. "Why do you always act this way?"

"Act what way?" Rita shot back.

"Like I'm some kind of jailor. I made rules to keep us all safe. When I moved us out here, I didn't expect you to stay. You could have gone at anytime."

"I don't mind living here, I just don't want you all up in my business. Besides, you know finding work is hard for me and with my credit getting a place is hard, too."

"Then why don't you move in with one of those guys you hang with then, huh? Probably because most of them live with their mothers or the mother of their children."

"This one's different," Rita said in a low voice. "He treats me good. I haven't had a man treat me like this in a long time."

"Who is he?"

"You met him a few times."

"Terrell? You're still seeing him?" Greta said surprised. She remembered a soft spoken man who liked wearing black jeans and smoked cigars. He'd lasted the longest. Nearly a year.

"Yes."

He was a little younger than her mother, but one of the most polite. He didn't say much but most of her mother's friends rarely did. He didn't look like trouble, but Greta had learned early that looks could be deceiving.

"Just be careful."

"I always am."

Greta forced a smile, knowing that wasn't true.

THE MOMENT VANCE opened the door to Sylvie's apartment she threw her arms around him. "I was so worried."

He held her close, inhaling her sweet perfume and sinking into her soft embrace. He tightened his hold, a part of him, the part of him he wanted to ignore, wishing he'd been able to do the same with Greta. He wished he could have hugged her and told her how sorry he was for the past. He wanted to tell her how much he'd enjoyed being with her last night. He squeezed his eyes closed wanting to erase the look of shock and hurt that had crossed her face before it turned to anger and indifference. He should have expected it. She would have put things together eventually. He just hadn't wanted to be there when she did. Damn. He liked her and she hated his guts.

She wasn't the only one. His mother was furious with him for missing the luncheon. He'd taken the taxi to the hospital to pick up his car and then driven around for awhile before going to Sylvie's place.

Sylvie drew away and looked up at him concerned. "What happened?"

He forced a smile. "I'm on Mom's bad son list."

She stroked his cheek. "You can't blame her for being upset. She hosts that luncheon only once a year and she expects her family to be there."

"I know. I feel bad enough. Fortunately she has my brother to turn to."

"I'll make it up to her for you."

Vance drew back, feeling annoyed. Sometimes he felt that Sylvie cared more about his mother's feelings than she did his. "I don't want to talk about the luncheon right now."

Her gaze grew serious. "Are you okay? How about that girl?"

Vance swallowed a lump in his throat and tried to make his voice sound casual. "She's fine. She was mugged. I stayed at the hospital longer than expected."

"Then you took her home," Sylvie finished. "I know, you told me." She grinned. "She must consider you her hero."

No, anything but. Vance pulled Sylvie close and kissed her, while unbuttoning her blouse. He wanted her. He didn't want to think. He just wanted to feel her soft body next to his. He wanted to feel her legs around him.

"Isn't it early for this?" she asked.

"It's never too early," he breathed against her neck.

She pulled off his shirt. "I'm glad you're all right."

"Never better," he lied.

GRETA STARED LISTLESSLY at the walls of the Red Hut and sighed. She didn't even know why she was there. It was one of Drake's restaurants. She didn't want to be home and didn't know where else to go, then the thought came to her to come there and bury her past for good. She'd have a great meal and then forget men for good. It was the evening rush, so the restaurant was buzzing with the wait staff coming in and out of the kitchen carrying trays loaded with savory Island dishes. Greta looked around. The other tables were filled with happy looking families and couples. *Some people were meant to be in pairs, she was meant to stay single.* She didn't mind being alone. She was used to it. Maybe, the next time she'd take her grandmother out, but for now, she wanted to deal with the thoughts that still haunted her. She wanted to remind herself of how foolish she'd been. She didn't want any more ghosts.

Greta sipped her drink then glanced up and her breath caught when she spotted another face from the past. A tall, dark, handsome man wearing gold rimmed glasses and a smile that could be a little wicked: Eric Henson. He walked past her table with a courteous nod and nothing more. She wasn't surprised. What man, or boy for that matter, remembered his first time, much less who he did it with? Greta set her glass down at the same time she heard his footsteps stop. He backed up and stared down at her. He then slid into the booth in front of her, rested his chin in his hands and a slow sexy grin spread on his face. It was the grin that did it. He remembered and as he stared at her a similar grin spread on her face and her cheeks grew warm. Now she remembered why she'd slept with him. He was very charming, and he had eyes that saw a lot more than expected.

"Greta Rodgers," he said, as if remembering a favorite meal.

"Eric Henson."

They both laughed, then he jumped to his feet and opened his arms. She hugged him, feeling as if she'd met an old friend, even though they'd hardly been that. It had been awkward but fun. She'd felt guilty for using him to get close to his brother. No doubt *he'd seduced her*. He was the type to do so. Seeing the man he'd become she guessed he was clever and unassuming.

"How are you doing?" he asked with a warmth that surprised her. His island lilt wasn't as strong as Drake's, but it was just as sexy.

"I'm fine."

Eric glanced at the bruise on her face. "Are you sure?"

"Yes, I was mugged last night."

His face changed. "Have you gone to the police?"

"I didn't need to, he didn't get anything."

His brows shot up. "You fought him off?"

"No, someone else helped me," Greta said not wanting to elaborate. "So how are you? What have you been up to? Do you work with your brother?"

"Yes, but I also have my own business. I'm a financial advisor."

"I'll remember that when I make more money."

"You don't need a lot. It pains me to see how many people just depend on their 401k and savings, not understanding the importance of investments, and being able to differentiate between net and gross. Financial literacy is essential. Too many people don't understand the logistics of how to make money work for them."

Greta held up her hands, as if in surrender. "Okay I'm convinced."

Eric laughed, then hung his head, embarrassed. "Sorry, it's a passion of mine."

"Passion is good. So, are you still breaking hearts?"

Eric adjusted his glasses then rested his arms on the table and lowered his voice. "That's Drake's territory, remember?"

"Is that still your MO, Mr. Five Seconds?" She'd called him that after their first time. He'd been overeager and quick. At least he'd been gentle and they'd learned together. She'd taught him to slow down.

Color stained his cheeks. "Twenty seconds at least."

Greta bit back a smile. "Not as I remember."

"I've improved."

"I'm sure you have."

Eric glanced to the door. "Drake's not here."

"That's okay, I'm not here to see him. I met him at the reunion and his wife."

Eric frowned. "His wife?"

"Cassie."

"Oh right, Cassie," he said, as if suddenly remembering.

Greta laughed. "Does he have another wife?"

Eric leaned back and folded his arms. "Sometimes I forget he has a wife at all."

"She seems nice."

"She's great."

Greta picked up her drink. She didn't want to discuss Drake's wife.

"So, are you expecting someone?"

"No, I just decided to check out this place on my own. I've heard good things about it. But I wouldn't mind the company."

He glanced up. "Sorry, I wish I could but my date's here."

Greta's heart sank, but she kept a smile on her face. "Oh, right. Enjoy yourself."

She didn't know whether it was her smile or her voice, but something made Eric stop and really look at her with an intensity that was unnerving. "Would you like to meet her? We could all—"

"No," Greta said quickly. Damn his eyes. Eric could read women better than any man should. "Three's a crowd as they say," she said with a forced chuckle. "It was just a thought."

He didn't smile, his brown eyes searching her face with a tenderness that brought tears to her eyes. "It's a nice thought," he said. "We'll do it another time."

Greta dropped her gaze to her drink. "Yes, sure," she said not wanting to see him again.

Eric turned to the waiter who'd approached Greta's table to take her order. "Everything is on me."

Her head shot up. "You don't have to."

He bent down and whispered in her ear. "I know." He straightened, then winked and left. She turned and saw him greet a young woman then leave the restaurant. The Henson brothers could shatter a woman's heart. How could men be so delicious and kind at the same time? No wonder they were both spoken for.

"Are you ready to order?" the waiter asked.

"Give me a few more minutes please."

"Sure."

Greta sank back in her seat feeling deflated. Strike three. Drake was married. Eric was involved and Vance. She didn't even want to think about Vance. Even if he didn't have a girl-friend, she couldn't imagine him being interested in her or she him. Her grandmother was definitely wrong. *There was to be no man from her past.* Her life was going to remain exactly the same.

"WHAT'S THIS? Who's Vance Minton?" Her grandmother asked a month later. She'd come over to help Greta with spring cleaning. It was an activity she enjoyed, although Greta found it more of a drudgery. All the windows were open to air out the house and allow the aromatic scent of flowers to seep through, as well as sunlight which brightened each room. They'd been dusting and polishing the living room when her grandmother had spotted a card underneath the couch.

Greta looked at the card, surprised by the sight of it. "Nothing. I thought I'd thrown it away."

"But there's a note on the back."

Greta reached for the card. She didn't remember seeing a note on it.

Her grandmother moved it out of reach and narrowed her eyes. "There's a story here."

"Not really."

"Stop lying," Rita said flopping down on the couch and switching on the TV. "You were salivating."

"No, I wasn't," Greta snapped.

Rita shook her head. "Mom, you should have seen her with this guy. He even called her Tera."

Her grandmother frowned at Greta. "What is she going on about?"

Rita rested her feet on the coffee table. "Some guy she picked up at the reunion."

Greta pushed her mother's feet off the table and bent down and scrubbed the marks with a rag.

"You didn't tell me about that," her grandmother said. "You said nothing happened."

"See Mom?" Rita said with a smirk. "I'm not the only one who lies around here."

"I wasn't lying," Greta said. "I didn't meet him at the reunion."

"Who is he?"

"Van the Man," Rita said in a sing songy voice. "And he used to go to her school."

"But you didn't meet him at the reunion?" her grandmother asked.

"No." Greta sighed, knowing she was trapped. Now she had to tell her grandmother the full story or her mother would invent her own version. Greta sat down on the love seat and patted a seat next to her for Minnie. She sat and listened while Greta told her about the incident with the flat tire, then the mugger, and how Vance had driven her home. "And then I invited him in for coffee and found out he has a girlfriend and that was it."

Rita shook her head. "No, you're leaving out the best part."

Greta gritted her teeth. "Mom, let it go."

"Don't you think your grandmother should know that you spent the night with him?"

"I didn't. I had taken some pain medicine they gave me at the hospital. It made me sleepy." Greta turned to her grandmother hoping she would believe her. "We both fell asleep on the couch."

"In each others' arms," Rita added.

"I somehow ended up with my head on his chest."

"And he had his arms around you."

Greta sent Rita a fierce glare. "It wasn't like that. But of course when it comes to men, everything is about sex."

Rita crossed her legs and licked her lips. "The best part."

Minnie turned to her daughter. "She isn't gutter like you, Rita."

Rita got up and went into the kitchen.

Greta rolled her eyes and returned her attention to her grandmother. "Anyway we woke up and he went back to his girlfriend."

Her grandmother stared down at the card in her hand. "And he gave you his card?"

"He was just being polite."

Rita shouted from the kitchen. "Don't be fooled by her Mom. Greta liked him until she remembered who he was. I knew who he was right away."

"No, you didn't."

"I almost did. I had a boyfriend back then who had a cousin or something on the boy's varsity basketball team, so I remembered him. Greta didn't. You should have seen her face."

Her grandmother looked at Greta. "Who was he?"

Greta stood and began to rub down a bookshelf. "I don't want to talk about it."

"Did he call you names or something?"

"Who didn't?" Rita scoffed returning to the living room eating a biscuit.

Minnie looked at her daughter. "Shut. Your. Mouth."

"This is my house too."

"Right, your name's written all over the deed," she said every word laced with sarcasm.

Rita kissed her teeth in annoyance. "I'm gone." She grabbed her purse and keys then left.

"Who is this man?" Minnie asked.

"Nobody. I thought at first maybe...but then...he has a girl-friend anyway so—"

"You're not making sense."

Greta slapped her cleaning rag against her thigh, desperate to change the subject. "There's nothing to make sense of."

"You liked him."

"Before I knew who he really was, yes, I did. I admit that."

"And he liked you." Her grandmother held up her hand when Greta opened her mouth to protest. "He wouldn't have come in for coffee and given you his number if he hadn't."

"You don't know this man. He had me call him Vance the whole time, just to deceive me, and I bet if I hadn't hit my head I would have put two and two together earlier. He probably just wanted a place to crash to get away for a while. It was nothing personal. 'Van the Man' is not a guy you can trust."

"Maybe he's no longer 'Van the Man'. Maybe he is just Vance now. We can all change."

"True," Greta said with a shrug. She waved her rag in the air as if offering him a royal pardon. "I wish him the best and that's the end of the story."

"Not quite," her grandmother said in a thoughtful tone.

"What do you mean?"

"I want you to see him again."

"Absolutely not!"

"Why not?"

Greta threw up her hands. "Because he's a jerk."

"That's not the man you described. I like the sound of him. He was considerate and fun and—"

"What happened that night was an anomaly. Trust me, he

doesn't want to see me, and I don't want to see him. I went to the class reunion just as you asked me to, and it was a disaster. I'm not setting myself up again."

"I told you to keep your heart open."

"Presently my heart is battered and bruised and needs a rest."

"He likes you and he may know somebody."

"He won't."

"Humor me. Do this one last thing for me and I won't ask anything of you again."

Greta sighed. "How am I supposed to see him again without looking completely pathetic?"

"This is what I want you to do. You are to go by his office with a gift of thanks. If he is rude, then you know you are right about him. But if he's not, the possibilities are endless. I just don't want you to paint a picture of a man you hardly know."

"But I do know him."

"You know who he used to be. This 'Van the ban—'"

"Man."

"Person. Your sister has changed. Is it fair for someone to use her past to judge her now?"

Greta stiffened, irritated by the comparison. "She's different."

"Because she's female?"

"I don't have a thing against guys."

"Then see him again. Prove me wrong. Show me how horrible he is. If it was all just an act then you'll know for sure, and you'll be able to throw this card away."

Her grandmother was right. She had been hanging onto the card for some strange reason. At first she'd had it resting on her counter, then she tossed it on the bookshelf then on the table, but she hadn't thrown it away. She'd held onto it, as if it meant something. Greta took the card and flipped it over. "There's no note here."

Her grandmother grinned. "But you thought there was."

"Okay," Greta said, ready to take on the challenge. "You want me to find out who he really is? You're on."

CHAPTER SIX

"So, when will I start hearing wedding bells?"

Vance looked up from his desk and stared at the man standing in the doorway. Cordell Aguilar, a big Latino man with dark skin and a Southern accent as thick as Texas chili, was the owner of CA Construction and Sylvie's father. Cordell was the father he wished he'd had. He was a savvy businessman who'd been a little ruthless in his youth (under-bidding his competition), but he was brilliant. At first Cordell had been suspicious of him, especially when he'd started dating Sylvie, but Vance had won him over with his work ethic and the respect of the other men. Within months, Cordell had taken Vance under his wing and helped him rise up the ranks.

After two years, Vance had started to save up enough money to buy out the business. It had been agreed upon based on a gentleman's handshake. Cordell promised him that once he married into the family the business would be his. Cordell was ready to retire, but wanted to keep the business in the family. He trusted Vance to run the operation and only balked at some suggestions he found too progressive. Cordell was very conservative when it came to change. He didn't visit the main office, unless he had something to say, and evidently today he did. Vance cleared a seat and gestured for Cordell to sit.

"This is a surprise," Vance said. "Want a drink?"

"I didn't come here for chit chat." He sat. "Answer my question."

"Hopefully next year."

"I don't believe in hope. It's either yes or no."

"I'll admit I haven't made it a top priority. Business has been booming and we have a lot of work."

"Son, I like making money, but I also like seeing my children happy and Sylvie isn't."

"She's not?"

"She told me you still have your own place. I told you I'd buy you two a house."

"I prefer we buy a house on our own."

"That's fine. I understand that, but you're together most of the time and have been for years, why keep your own place?"

"I use it like a separate office sometimes. It's another place where I can think."

"A man shouldn't work too hard or waste time. If you plan to start a family you'd better start soon."

"You're right."

Cordell folded his arms. "I want to see an engagement ring on my baby's finger in three months or less. Then we'll begin planning a wedding. Clear?"

"Yes, sir."

He beamed. "Good." Cordell stood and patted Vance on the back. "I knew you just needed a little nudge." He went over to the window. "You've made my business more lucrative than I could have imagined. I'm going to be proud handing my daughter over to you." He glanced out the window then chuck-led. "Good Lord, what is that?"

"What?"

"You've got to come see this."

Vance walked over to the window and looked out. He froze. It was Greta. She was dressed in a bright paisley top and black skirt. Her large glasses reflected the sun making them look like saucers and her hair was an untamable mess the wind toyed with. Greta struggled to balance the large potted plant she carried.

"She looks like Dustin Hoffman in the movie *Tootsie*," Cordell said with a laugh. "But at least he was in fashion back then."

Vance shot him a look. "Don't make fun of her."

"Why not? I thought only women over eighty wore glasses like that." He laughed harder, wiping tears from his eyes.

Vance turned from the window, trying to get his thoughts in order. What was she doing here? It had been a month since that night and he thought he'd never see her again. Why was he so happy at the prospect? He rolled down his sleeves and straightened his shirt. "I'm serious, Aguilar. Stop laughing."

Cordell looked at him surprised. "Why? You know her or something?"

Vance cleared up his desk. "Yes, she's a friend."

"Really? You know her?"

Vance gritted his teeth annoyed by Cordell's disbelief. "Yes."

"Sorry, I didn't realize she was a client."

"She's not. I met her several nights ago."

"Oh," he said slowly, as if finally coming to an under-standing ."So you didn't see what she looked like until now.

You were drunk right and gave her the wrong impression. Want me to get rid of her for you?"

"No." Vance searched for a tie and quickly put it on.

Cordell watched him amazed. "What you getting dressed up for?"

"No reason." His hands were trembling too much. He yanked the tie off and shoved it in a draw. He had to be cool. Maybe she wasn't coming to see him. There were other offices in the building. Maybe... His phone rang and he reached for the receiver so fast he knocked over a cup of pencils. "There's a Greta Rodgers to see you without an appointment," his receptionist said.

"Fine. Give me a minute then send her in." Vance set the phone down then picked up the pencils. He could feel Cordell's eyes watching him.

"I've never seen you this jumpy before."

He replaced the pencils back then set the cup on the desk. "I'm not jumpy."

"What does this woman mean to you?"

Damned if he knew. "I helped her after a mugging."

"Oh yes, Sylvie told me about that."

There was a light knock on the door.

"Come in," Vance said.

His receptionist opened the door and Greta came in carrying the large palm plant. Vance saw Cordell bite back a laugh and saw his receptionist look Greta up and down as if she were a joke. Heat rose up his neck. He jumped up from his chair and took the plant from her. He set it in the corner and wiped his hands, annoyed that she wasn't aware of how others saw her. "Why the hell didn't you just have this delivered? You could have hurt yourself."

"It's not that heavy, Vance. It's just awkward. I thought

you'd like it. It's easy to care for and will help the air quality of your office. It's a thank you gift."

Vance rested his hands on his hips, avoiding Cordell's gaze. He knew his boss had been surprised by Greta referring to him as "Vance", especially since he didn't let anyone else do so. She had some dirt on her skirt and a smudge on her cheek and he thought she looked adorable. He was so happy to see her he didn't know what to do. "You didn't have to go through all that trouble."

"It wasn't. I'll just—"

"His manners aren't always the best," Cordell said. "What you did was real kind."

She smiled at him. "Thank you."

Vance stepped forward. "Cordell, this is my friend Tera. Tera, my boss, Cordell Aguilar."

"And future father-in-law," he added. "I won't keep you any longer, Van." He opened the door. "A pleasure to meet you, Tera." He looked at Vance and wiggled his fingers. "And remember what I expect to see." He left.

Greta looked at the closed door and swung her arms as if she didn't know what to do next. "I guess that's my cue too."

Vance leaned against the door blocking her. "No, I want you to stay."

Greta paused. She hadn't expected to be alone with him. She'd imagined dropping off the plant and getting a cold reception, then calling Minnie and triumphing at her victory. Instead, she was looking up into intense brown eyes in the face of a man she wanted to hate but couldn't anymore. Her grandmother was right, he wasn't 'Van the Man' anymore. Van would never ask her to stay. Van would never look at her like this. She bit her lip. "Sorry about the other day."

Vance shrugged. "Sorry, I didn't tell you the truth."

Greta looked around the office. "You're doing very well for yourself." She looked at a picture on the wall. "Is that the Bartholdi Fountain?"

Vance came up behind her, almost close enough to touch. "Yes," he said impressed. "Most people don't know that." He lowered his voice and his tone turned wistful. "I love fountains. Especially the sculptures that surround them."

Greta turned to him, startled by his nearness, but she didn't move back. "Then you must love looking at the Court of Neptune Fountain, it's near the Library of Congress."

His gaze held hers. "Yes, and I also love going to the Dupont Circle Fountain."

Greta swallowed and gripped her hands together basking in the warm glow of his gaze. "Have you been to the McMillian Fountain?"

"No. Where is it? Show me."

Greta walked over to his desk. "I think they have a 3D view online. I'll do a search for you—"

"No, I mean take me there."

"Now?"

"Do you have something else to do?"

It was the end of the day and she was off work. "No," Greta said feeling a little off balance. She hadn't expected an invitation to spend time with him.

They drove in separate cars, since Greta insisted. Vance had his receptionist order a packed meal from his favorite Deli, which he picked up on the way, and met Greta at McMillian Reservoir, located in the Bloomingdale neighborhood of Washington. Greta was in shock when she opened the picnic basket. It was filled with succulent, fresh strawberries, several hard cheeses, turkey and ham slices, croissants, whipped butter, and several French fruit tarts for dessert. And, of course, a delicate white wine was included, along with long-stem plastic wine glasses. They selected a place close by the fountain, where Greta spread out a decorative woolen blanket she'd pulled out of the trunk of her car.

"Wow, are you always this prepared?" she asked.

"I'm always prepared for a picnic. Especially, if there's a fountain nearby." Vance looked up at the structure. "You're right. This fountain is amazing. I've never heard about this one." It was a beautiful bronze fountain, consisting of three large figures called The Three Graces, mounted upon a pink granite base.

"I wonder what they're for," Vance said, pointing to the figures.

Greta adjusted her glasses. "The 'Three Graces' are there to help provide onlookers with a sense of honor, serenity and virtue."

Vance tilted his head, studying her. "How do you know so much about the fountain?"

"My family didn't go on holidays or trips, so I would go to the library and look up different places to visit, aside from museums, I liked to look at sculptures and fountains, so I'd find out as much as I could about them and then take myself on an outing. When my niece lived with me, I used to take her with me. She loved playing and throwing coins into the water."

"I love the sound of the water," he said in a quiet voice. "I find it soothing."

Greta watched him, curious. He seemed in awe but there was also a sadness she couldn't understand. She'd caught a glimpse of it when he was in his office, just after his boss had left. For some reason his expression reminded her of a man she'd met years ago. There had been abject sadness in his eyes. She was sixteen and had gone to the local food pantry to get some groceries to fill up their empty kitchen cupboards. Although she had an afterschool job, their finances were tight.

Her mother's employment was spotty, and while Marlene was out of school, she rarely worked complaining that she had to take care of Brianna. Greta was putting a loaf of bread in her basket when she looked up and saw an older man walking down the aisle, as if in a daze. He was tall with features that hinted of a West African background. She'd prided herself on knowing the difference between African Americans, those from the Caribbean, and Africans that filled her neighborhood.

He was well dressed, but his eyes looked haunted. She'd seen men in many states—intoxication, high, depressed but something about his expression worried her. It wasn't like the rest.

"Sir, can I help you?"

His dark brown gaze met hers. "I don't know what to do," he said in a thick lyrical accent. "I never thought I'd find myself in a place like this."

Greta knew some people felt ashamed coming to the pantry, but she had no such problem. "It's not hard. Let me help you. How many people do you have in your family?"

"Five. Including myself."

"Do you have any babies or toddlers?"

"No. Two adults and three children." He lifted up a can and looked at the label. "Most of the food here is so strange to me. I don't understand them."

Greta nodded understanding. Her grandmother had once mentioned how, when she first arrived in the U.S., her number one job was to find a local Caribbean store so that she could buy foods familiar to her. Unfortunately, since he was in the pantry she knew he probably wouldn't be able to afford to go anywhere else. Greta searched her mind and knew which items to suggest. Soups and casseroles had served her well, because they could stretch ingredients and be frozen.

Greta wondered why his wife wasn't there helping him, then decided she must have to stay home with the children. She rarely found men at the pantry getting food for their families. Although he was a large man, there was a gentleness about him that she'd never seen in an African before. Most of the Africans she had been exposed to were either arrogant, or they were abrupt, and at times abrasive. He was different.

Greta led the man around, up and down the aisles and explained the different food items. She picked up a can of chili. "This is made of kidney beans and ground beef. It's quick and you just freeze it and then heat it up." Next she made sure he selected several cans of tomato sauce "Your wife can use this when making a sauce or soup." Soon his basket was filled with cans of soup, corn, a variety of beans, and tuna. She made sure to include several loaves of bread and rolls, and of course, several ripe apples. "Now, don't worry. You'll be okay," she told him as they left the pantry. "I'm sure your wife will be pleased with your selection. The beans are a great source of protein, so you don't need to add any meat, and you have all she'll need to make some hearty soups and stew for the family."

The man turned and looked at her. "You're a beautiful little angel."

Greta laughed. No one had ever called her an angel, let alone beautiful. She envied his family. His kids were lucky to have a father like him. For the first time in a long while she dreamed of having a different family life. "Glad I could help."

He pointed at her. "Continue to do well in your studies and you'll go far. Make your parents proud. I wish I had a daughter like you."

And she wished she had a father like him, but she didn't

say so. Instead, Greta said goodbye then watched him catch a bus. She'd met him at the pantry several more times, and she would help him fill his basket. She even wrote down some simple recipes for his wife. Then one day he never returned. Greta thought of that man now, as she looked at Vance.

She didn't know why she could easily recognize distress or pain in others. Perhaps it was because she'd felt so much of it in her life. She didn't know why, but she wanted whatever was bothering him to go away. Greta excused herself, telling Vance she needed to use the restroom, then disappeared into a souvenir shop across the street and bought him a small ornament of the fountain.

Several minutes later Greta returned and after lying down on the blanket, handed Vance the gift.

Vance took the gift out of the bag. "What's this for?"

"An early wedding gift."

"Thank you." He held it up then set it down in his lap. "It won't be until next year. I haven't even bought her an engagement ring yet."

"So her father is getting ahead of himself?"

"No." Vance bit his lip and glanced at a passing jogger.

"You're not ready yet?"

"I thought I was. I mean, I should be. Sylvie and I have been dating for years and..." He shook his head. "Cordell is right, I've been waffling too long. I've been focusing on the business and I need to put other priorities first." He clapped his hands together. "I know. Let's go look at some rings."

"You like to do things on impulse, don't you?" Greta said, watching Vance begin to put the items away.

"Not usually. Since coming to work for Cordell I've been very structured. I have to be, there are so many things I have to think about. So many people I have to work with."

"Going to the reunion was an impulsive decision, wasn't it?"

"How do you know?"

"If you'd thought it through, you would have arrived early with your gorgeous girlfriend on your arm for everyone to see."

"How do you know she's gorgeous?"

Greta raised a brow. "I don't think you've changed that much."

Vance laughed. "You're right. Getting Sylvie was a real coup for me."

"For her too, I'm sure."

"Hmm. You're right, going to the reunion was impulsive. I felt like I was getting stuck in a rut and I wanted to do something different."

"I know the feeling, except it was my grandmother who urged me to go. But I discovered that I no more fit in now than I did back then."

"I'm glad you went. I wouldn't have gotten a chance to really know you."

Greta laughed. "You think that was worth a flat tire and time spent in an emergency room?"

"Yes. You remind me of things I've forced myself to neglect. I've lived in or near this city all my life, and I've never taken the time to come here." He held up the souvenir. "Thanks for giving me a second chance."

"You too."

Vance put the souvenir away. "I'm glad we didn't meet at the reunion." His gaze lifted and captured hers. "I doubt we would have gotten to know each other like this. Now, we're friends."

Greta stared at him, startled by the thought. "We are?"

He gestured to the food and the surroundings. "What do you call this?"

"Okay," she laughed sheepishly. She'd hoped for it, but hadn't allowed herself to believe that it could be true. "I guess you're right."

"So, you have to help me."

"Do what?"

"Choose an engagement ring for Sylvie."

Greta jerked her head back. "I can't help you do that."

"Why not?"

"Because I don't even know her. How will I know what she'll like?"

"I'll tell you all about her on the way there. I'm driving and I'll pay for the long term parking for your car." He didn't allow for any discussion.

"Okay."

Greta didn't feel comfortable shopping with Vance to find a ring for his fiancé, but she did enjoy being with him. Sylvie was a lucky woman and probably knew it. They drove into Virginia and found a small jewelry store. Vance looked over every ring with care and asked her opinion. Greta watched him and imagined him proposing, and could see that while the arrogant boy had gone, there were still hints of him present. Vance liked to get his own way, and used his looks to his advantage, he knew she'd go with him, but he was also the man she remembered from that night over a month ago.

"I like it," Greta said assessing the diamond ring he held up. "I think you've found the one."

Vance sighed frustrated, returned the ring and continued looking at others. "I'm not sure yet."

Greta lightly rested her hand on his arm. "You'll find the one."

He glanced down at her hand. "You have nice fingers. Maybe if you try one on."

Greta snatched her hand back. "No."

Her reaction amused him. "Why not?"

She hid her hands behind her back. "Because I don't want to."

"I thought we were friends."

"My answer's still no."

A teasing glint of humor lit his eyes. "Come on, Tera," he urged in a low, coaxing voice. "It would be good practice for both of us. One day, a guy is going to slide a ring on your finger. Don't you want to know how it feels?"

"I don't need to practice. When he does, I want him to be the only one."

"You're a romantic," he said with feigned disappointment.

"No, I'm not. It's just bad luck."

"Says who?"

Greta threw up her hand in exasperation. "Somebody. Somewhere. This is a momentous act that should only be between you and Sylvie."

"Yes, I was right." Vance tweaked her chin. "You're a romantic." He turned to the glass case and pointed to another ring. "I would like to look at those?" The jeweler opened the back of the display and removed a tray of rings. He placed the tray on the counter.

"I'm not a romantic."

He didn't look at her. "You can deny it all you want, but I know the truth."

She narrowed her gaze. "Okay, you want to pretend?" She wrapped her hands around his arm and cuddled up close to him like an excited teenager with a new boyfriend.

He stiffened. "What are you doing?"

"Pretending to be Sylvie." She reached up and playfully kissed him on the cheek. "Oh Van this is such a wonderful surprise," she said imitating a thick Southern accent to match Cordell's. "I've dreamed of this moment for so long. Aren't these rings so pretty? I really like that big one over there."

The corner of Vance's mouth quirked with humor. "She wouldn't act like that."

"Oh, sorry, I'll add more sophistication." Greta deepened her tone, lifted her chin and loosened her grip on his arm. "Oh darling aren't those exquisite?" She pointed to another ring set.

Vance shook his head. "She never calls me 'darling'."

"Never?"

"Nope."

"Honey?"

He shook his head.

Greta casually looped her arm through his, then gestured to different selection. "Okay, Bartie, how about this one?"

"Bartie?"

"Yes, short for Bartholdi, the fountain you love and have on your wall. That's what I'd call you, if you were mine." She pushed up her glasses, embarrassment making her cheeks hot. "But you're not," she quickly added, letting her hands fall to her sides. "So it doesn't matter. See, I told you I wasn't romantic. I'm sure Sylvie calls you something better than that."

Vance stared at her for a long moment, his eyes darkening with an emotion she couldn't read, then he abruptly turned. "Let's get out of here."

"But you haven't selected anything," Greta said hurrying to keep up with him.

"I will later," he replied in a curt tone.

She shrugged. "Fine. But did my little charade help you at least a little?"

He opened the car and got in the driver's seat.

Greta got into the passenger seat and looked at him with unease, her stomach in knots. "You're angry. Okay, what did I do wrong? I wasn't trying to make fun of Sylvie. I'm sure she's wonderful."

Vance started the ignition. "I'm not angry."

Greta turned it off. "Yes, you are. Vance, please. We can't be friends if you're not honest with me."

He stared out the window. "I'm angry at myself. Not you." He turned to her. "I thought getting the ring would be easier and I feel like I've failed. I'm just tired."

Greta visibly relaxed. "I understand. Don't be too hard on yourself. It's a big step and I know you want it to be perfect. But I bet that any ring you get Sylvie will be perfect because she'll be marrying you. And that's all that matters."

Vance groaned, then pulled out of the parking lot.

"What's the groan for?"

His smile was boyishly affectionate. "You're so sweet."

Greta shook her head. "First you called me a 'romantic' and now I'm 'sweet'. You don't know me at all."

"Yes, I do." He nudged her with his elbow. "Better than you think."

That was what scared her. Greta knew he was right. And she felt as if she knew him too, on a deep level. She'd hit a nerve in the jewelry store, she just didn't know what. She'd seen a little bit of wistfulness and sadness, but she couldn't figure out why. She would be more careful with her teasing, his friendship meant a lot to her. It wasn't his fault she had stronger feelings for him than he did for her. "Well, take your time. Don't let this be too much of a pressure, it's unhealthy."

Vance raised a brow, amused. "Are you worrying about me again?"

"No, just offering a little advice. I'm sure when I get back from my trip you can tell me all about the perfect ring you found for her."

Vance turned sharply to her. "Where are you going?"

"I have to travel for work. Rhode Island."

"How long?"

"Two weeks."

He nodded, as if carefully processing the information. "When you get back, call me. I'd like you to meet Sylvie."

CHAPTER SEVEN

Vance drove home, gripping the steering wheel tighter than he needed to and with his AC on full blast. He needed to cool down. He looked at the jacket on the passenger seat Greta had accidentally left it in his car. He then glanced at the souvenir she had given him. He'd hung it on his rearview mirror. She was back in his life and it felt good—too damn good. His mood dipped as he thought about Cordell's visit and shopping for rings. He didn't know why he couldn't just settle on one. He knew Sylvie would like whatever he picked out for her.

A smiled touched his mouth as he remembered Greta asking the jeweler to get them the rings they wanted to look at. She didn't care about the surprised glances sent her way, she carried herself as if she were the CEO of a Fortune 500 company. During their picnic at the fountain he'd been fascinated about her work as Senior Physicist at the Environmental Protection Agency and knew she'd worked hard to get there. She was genuine and real. Yes, it had been light and easy fun until she'd pretended to be Sylvie, and given him a nickname.

He drummed his fingers on the steering wheel. She was going to Rhode Island for two weeks and he missed her already. Maybe that was how it was with a new friendship. He hit the steering wheel and swore. Who the hell was he fooling, he liked her. A lot more than he should. Twice, at the fountain, he'd wanted to touch her cheek when the wind blew her hair into her face. He liked the smell of her lotion and felt himself respond when she brushed against him, in the jewelry store, and wrapped her fingers around his arm, pretending to be his girlfriend.

Why couldn't he get her out of his mind? Why did he feel this way? He'd finally gotten his life exactly the way he wanted. He worked for a booming business, had important clients, good friends, a sexy girlfriend and the car he'd always dreamed he would have and yet... And yet he felt restless, as if something was missing. But what could be missing? He'd worked hard to bury the boy he'd been to become the man he was. The boy Greta remembered. God what was wrong with him? Why had he been so happy to see her again? Why had her nickname touched him deep to the core? Why couldn't he stop thinking about her?

Vance turned up the radio and rolled down his window.

It was no big deal. He just admired her. He admired her courage and spirit. He liked that she hadn't made fun of his love of fountains and had bought him a plant for his office. He even liked how she handled her mother. It amazed him that no matter how coarse or cutting her mother was, she deflected whatever she said with a nonchalance that amazed him. She'd done the same in school. She'd responded to taunts as if they were as important as gnats. It had amazed him that words that would have infuriated him didn't bother her.

That was it. He had a new friend he admired. He had a

terrific girlfriend, and a great life. He wouldn't do anything to jeopardize it.

When he got home Vance found Sylvie painting her toe nails in the living room. He bent down and kissed her.

"You're late. Long day?"

"No, a friend took me to see this amazing fountain. I'd like to take you there this weekend."

"Where?"

"It's The McMillian Fountain."

"Where is it?"

"In the Bloomingdale neighborhood."

"Oh, no. Are we back to that again?" She shook her head and chuckled. "I'd thought you'd gotten over your fountain craze. I remember you used to talk about all the fountains you'd love to visit, and how you plan to have one in our house one day."

Vance's good mood faded. "It's not a craze. Fountains are just things I find beautiful."

Sylvie fluttered her eyes at him. "So I'm not beautiful enough?"

He forced a smile. "Yes, I just...never mind."

She wiggled her toes. "Do you like this color? I think it's too light. I think I'll have to start over."

"It's fine."

"Or maybe I'll just go and get a professional pedicure." She put the nail polish aside.

"Sylvie, please let me take you there," he said. He desperately wanted to feel the same way he did with Greta, with her. He lightly touched her cheek. "You'll like it. We can have a picnic."

She kissed him on the cheek then stood. "If you really want to take me out, you need to think of some place more romantic." She slipped into a pair of pink flip-flops, turned and left.

He was getting married. She had to remember that. She was just his friend. That's all he saw. Greta put her clarinet away and sighed. She'd called him Bartie. She must have sounded like an idiot. She clicked her clarinet case closed. The rehearsal had gone well tonight, but she hadn't been as focused as she usually was. Going to Rhode Island was a blessing. She needed space from him. She'd proven her grandmother right, and made herself miserable.

"So what's his name?"

Greta turned to Joan Anderson, an older woman with honeyed skin, slick red hair and cat glasses who played first clarinet. "I'm sorry?"

"You were distracted tonight. I doubt it's work so it must be a man."

"We're just friends. I met him at my class reunion." *Sort of.*

"What does he do?"

"He's a contractor."

Joan laughed. "No, really, what does he do?"

"I just told you."

"He's a contractor?"

"Yes, he's very successful."

"I didn't expect that for you. I thought you'd find someone who would be more your intellectual equal. I know it's hard to find many black American men of our caliber, and that's why I don't limit my scope."

"I'm not limiting anything. I really like him and he's smart. Besides, as I said, we're just friends. He's engaged."

Her friend began to smile. "He's cute, isn't he?"

"Why do you say that?"

"Because that would explain why you'd be with someone less educated than you. We'll see if it lasts. Have your fun, but I guarantee you'll get bored."

Greta held up her hand. "Let me say this slowly: We. Are. Just. Friends."

"But you really like him. Have you told him?"

"I'm sorry, did you or did you not hear me tell you he's engaged."

"How long?" Joan asked.

"He's going to ask her soon. We went ring shop—"

"He took you shopping for rings?"

"Because I'm his friend. It's what friends do."

"Or maybe he's just clueless."

"You're being a snob."

"Says the woman who gets her love advice from her grandmother."

"She's a good judge of character." Greta knew that Joan didn't know anything about her background and she had only briefly mentioned Minnie telling her to go to the reunion, she kept that information to herself. She didn't want anyone privy to the drama of her life. At work she could be somebody else. She could pretend she went on family vacations to Vermont every spring, and took trips to the beach in the summer. She'd started pretending in college, never revealing what her family was really like. Her parents had divorced, her mother struggled as a single mother and, that was all she would share. She liked to listen to others tell about their extended family, three cars, charge cards and weekend trips to their cabins, lives that all seemed so foreign to her.

"Would he come to something like this?" Joan said, referring to one of their performances.

Probably not. "I don't need him to." She closed her case and stood. "Excuse me."

Joan was a good wake up call, Greta thought as she left. She and Vance did create an odd pair. It could never be something more than a simple friendship, he knew it and she did too. She would come back from Rhode Island, see the engagement ring on Sylvie's finger and realize that she had to accept that her life would never be that.

Greta was walking to her car when her cell phone rang. "Hello?"

"I want to stop by and give you back your jacket."

She'd totally forgotten about it. She could tell him to keep it until after her trip. She shouldn't see him again, but instead of listening to her rational mind, her heart took over. "Okay. I'll be home in about an hour. See you then." She disconnected then ran to her car, knowing she only needed twenty minutes to get home, but she wanted to be prepared. Just one more day then she'd fall back down to earth.

VANCE STOOD outside Greta's door and took a deep breath before he knocked. He should have waited until after her trip, but he'd wanted to see her before she left and he had to get rid of her jacket. He'd placed it in the trunk, but it didn't stop him from thinking about her. This was the only way to create the distance he needed.

She opened the door with a bright smile. "Hi, come in."

He stepped inside, knowing he should have just given her the jacket and left.

"Would you like anything to drink?"

"Juice would be fine."

Greta took the jacket from him and hung it up in the closet. "Just sit down and I'll be right back," she said, then disappeared into the kitchen.

Vance sat down and saw that her clarinet was out and a music book open. "You were practicing?" he asked, when she handed him his drink.

"Yes. I wasn't my best at rehearsal tonight."

He stood and walked over to her music stand. "It's a beautiful instrument."

Greta picked it up so he could have a closer look. "Thank you." She ran her fingers lightly over it. "I really saved up for it. Most of my life I had to play on plastic ones until I was able to afford wood. The detailing is amazing."

"I can see that."

"Go sit down, and I'll play something for you."

Vance returned to his seat and Greta adjusted the stand and grabbed a chair, then sat down. She flipped through her music book and selected a song. She licked her lips, forcing Vance to focus on her mouth. He watched her as she moistened the tip of the clarinet.

He cleared his throat and shifted in his seat, feeling oddly turned on. "What are you doing?"

"I have to get the reed wet enough, it gets dry quickly."

Vance watched her wet the reed and soon all he could think about was her warm, wet tongue wetting him then giving him a good blow just as she was about to do to the clarinet. He jumped up, startling her. "Sorry, I've got to go," he said looking at his watch instead of her shocked expression. "I just remembered something."

"Okay," Greta said, quickly recovering from his abrupt

change. She followed him to the door. "I'll play for you another time then."

No, he'd never let that happen. Vance opened the door and raced to his car. "Have a safe trip," he called over his shoulder, knowing the situation was too dangerous to look back.

SOMEHOW SHE'D FAILED AGAIN. Greta closed her front door and returned her clarinet to its case. What had happened? At first he'd sounded eager to have her play, then the next moment he was running out of her house. Maybe he was afraid she was going to play a classical piece he couldn't recognize and be bored to death. Perhaps Joan was right. She should try to get a man who would appreciate music. Someone she could play for and who would attend her orchestra performances.

Maybe Vance really had to do something else he'd forgotten about. Greta wanted to believe him, but she didn't. She put her clarinet case and music stand aside. All the signs were there. He had another life that didn't involve her. She would go to Rhode Island and let her foolish feelings run their course and then be sensible again.

She heard a car door slam then giggling. Greta looked out the window and saw her mother and Terrell making out against his car. In seconds they would look indecent; she knew her mother was brazen enough to make love to a man on the hood of his car. Greta grabbed her keys, pointed them in the direction of her car in the driveway and turned the alarm on. They immediately pulled apart.

"Oh, sorry," Greta said, rushing to her car. She jumped inside and turned the alarm off. She got out of the car and nodded at Terrell, wondering what trouble he was involved with. "Hi."

He nodded back, but Rita ignored her and gave him one last lingering kiss then drew away. "See you later, baby."

Terrell slapped her butt then got into his car and drove away.

Rita walked up to the house. "You're home early."

"No, you're just late."

Once inside, Rita set her purse on the coffee table and sat in front of the TV then sniffed the air. She turned to Greta. "You had a man here, didn't you?"

She froze. "What?"

Rita grinned, then sniffed the air some more. "I can always tell a man's cologne. And this man smells good."

"It was just someone returning my jacket."

"See, you should have been putting a jacket on him and getting yourself some."

Greta sighed. "Condoms and sex. Your level of interests astounds me."

"Don't be getting into a mood because you're sad and lonely."

"I'm not lonely," Greta said going to her room. But she was sad.

A week later, Vance returned to the office, after a hectic day submitting bids on three different lucrative projects. He sank in his chair and opened the drawer where Sylvie's ring sat. He picked up the small jewelry box and opened it. He was pleased with his purchase; a ring, with a thin band made of white gold, with diamonds surrounding a brilliant emerald stone. *Greta*

would like the colors. He smiled at the thought of showing her. *But the ring wasn't for her.* Vance snapped the box closed and shoved it back in the drawer.

His cell phone rang. He glanced at the number then picked up. "Hello?"

"I'm sending you a photo," Greta said. "Tell me what you think,"

Vance looked at the picture of the Court of Neptune Fountain in DC. "Wow that's incredible."

"I know. I was browsing the internet and I saw it and immediately thought of you. I dug up these pictures I took when I was there. It's a great fountain to see in person, up close. I wish you could see it for real."

"Me too." He wished he was there with her.

"You and Sylvie have to make plans to go there one day. I'm sending you some more pictures."

Vance looked at another picture of Greta sitting at the base of the fountain. He barely noticed the fountain—all he focused on was her. He traced her smile with his finger then he noticed how her top dipped low and he could see her cleavage. Her skin looked so smooth and soft. He still remembered the scent of her skin. He felt himself grow hard. He'd had the same response when they'd been in the jewelry store, and when she was getting ready to play her clarinet. He swore. He didn't just want to be with her. He wanted her.

"Did you get them?" she asked.

Vance rubbed his face, feeling torn. He loved hearing her voice and he didn't want their conversation to end, but it had to stop. "Yes, I have to go."

"What's wrong?"

He picked up a pencil one by one, and dropped them back into their holder. "Nothing."

"Friends are supposed to be honest with each other, right?"

"Yes."

"Then why are you lying to me?"

Vance briefly closed his eyes, searching for the right response. He really had to get off the phone, he just couldn't tell her why. "I bought Sylvie's ring."

"Are you nervous that she won't like it?"

He'd never been nervous asking a woman for anything. "Hmm."

"You'll be fine. Let me tell you what's going to happen. You're going to show her the ring and she's going to cry with joy and then," her voice cracked and her words died away.

"Are you okay?"

"I'm fine," she said in a voice too bright to be genuine.

Vance felt his heart pick up speed and he tightened his grip on the phone, wondering if she felt the same attraction he did. There was something in her voice he hadn't heard before. "And then what?" he asked in a soft tone.

"You'll get married and be very happy. Now, I'll let you go. Bye."

"Bye."

Vance tossed his phone down, depressed and annoyed with himself for feeling so. What the hell had he expected her to say? He stood and paced the room. He glanced at the corner where he'd removed the large potted plant she'd given him. He'd taken it out of his office and put it in his apartment. Every time he looked at it, he remembered the day she'd brought it to him. The day she'd come back into his life. He rested the flat of his hands on his desk and took a deep breath. This wasn't good. He knew he was in trouble.

GRETA WAS glad to be home. It had been a grueling trip, but she had to admit, she'd missed Vance. The two weeks hadn't lessened her feelings for him as she'd hoped. She'd almost given herself away on the phone when she was talking to him about the engagement ring he bought for Sylvie. But she'd pressed to find out what was wrong with him. She could tell, by his voice, that something was bothering him and he'd shared the truth: He loved his girlfriend so much he was nervous about asking her to marry him, afraid she'd say no. He didn't seem the type to have that kind of anxiety, but why would he lie about it?

Greta knew then what her next step would be. She had to meet Sylvie. She had to see Vance and Sylvie together so that she could see the love and commitment between them. It would be painful, but she had to face the truth. She'd invite Vance and Sylvie over for lunch and then never call him again. Staying friend would be too painful. Greta took her luggage out of her trunk and walked up the steps to her front door. She put her key in the lock and turned the door knob. She opened the door and screamed.

CHAPTER EIGHT

Greta knew immediately what had happened. There had been a police raid. Inside her house looked like a bomb had gone off. In the living room, nothing was spared. The carpet was ripped up, and several of the wooden floor planks were pulled up. They had pulled away some of the wallpaper, looking for 'hidden' places. She knew the drill, she had witnessed two drug busts by the age of eighteen, while living with her mother.

Her beloved couch, which she had inherited from Minnie, had been totally torn up, with all the stuffing and upholstery torn and ripped. Using crow bars, hacksaws and hammers the police had crudely pulled away some of the wood paneling she prized that covered one wall. An antique roll-top desk, where she kept her bills and papers, was open and all the contents were strewn on the floor. Even her clarinet case had been destroyed.

She rushed to the basement, where the floor tiles were dug up. They'd punched holes in the walls, leaving broken pieces of sheetrock in heaps on the floor. They must have found a stash of drugs hidden there, and decided to pry up the entire basement. Greta was too stunned to cry, as her anger continued to grow. She raced back up the stairs and ran out to the porch. They had done the most damage to the back of the house. The ceiling tiles in the covered patio had all been pulled down and broken. All the detailed original woodwork she loved so much had been pulled away and now lay in pieces. The screen door was crudely pulled off its hinges, and thrown aside.

Box cutters or sharp knives had been used to tear into the new patio furniture Greta had just bought last years, including all the stuffed pillows. They didn't even take the time to unzip them, they just cut them open. In the kitchen, each cabinet was thrown open and items were thrown on the floor. It was apparent they must not have found any drugs there, but not before pulling several cabinets from the wall. Her bedroom was also ransacked. Only the bathroom was spared.

Fuming Greta marched into her mother's bedroom and found her lying on the bed. Her bedroom was also torn up, from top to bottom. A built-in bookcase had been pried from the wall and they had cut through both mattresses. Incredibly, her mother hadn't even bothered to try and clean up anything. Instead, she'd just thrown a stained sheet over the mattress, which she was lying on, and had stacked her clothing on her mirrored dresser. She stubbed out a cigarette. "I didn't hear you come in."

Greta fought to keep her voice level. Her mother wasn't supposed to smoke inside the house, but evidently that wasn't the only rule she'd decided to break. Greta pointed to the door. "What happened to my house?" Greta tried to stay calm, but couldn't help shouting.

Rita sat up and held out her hands. "It was a mistake."

"The police came here by mistake?"

"No."

"What happened? This was a drug raid, wasn't it?" She waved her hands. "That was a rhetorical question, I already know the answer."

Rita jumped up. "I have a headache and I don't want to talk about it right now." She brushed past Greta and left the room.

Greta followed her down the hall. "You will talk about it." She grabbed her mother's arm and spun her around to face her. "Did this happen because of Terrell?"

Rita stared back, but soon let her gaze fall. "I'm sorry, baby."

"You let him stay here, didn't you?"

"I didn't see the harm in it. He was so sweet to me and he never caused any trouble."

"So, every time I had to travel for my job, you let him use my house to stash his drugs."

"I'm sorry, okay? When I gave him a key, I didn't know he'd been coming and hiding his dope here."

Greta's temper flared. "You gave him a key to my house?"

"He treated me so good, baby. All he needed was a place to sleep from time to time. And you'd go away on your trips and we have the space, so I couldn't say no to him."

Greta's body trembled with rage and her breath burned in her throat. "And you didn't think it was strange that he always decided to stay with you when I was out of town?"

"I was too busy enjoying having the house to ourselves. But you don't have to worry. I learned my lesson. He's being charged with drug possession, so I won't be seeing him anymore."

Greta stared at her mother so furious she could hardly

speak. Her mother acted as if the drug raid was comparable to spilling red wine on a white carpet. She was clueless. Greta walked passed her. "I'm through with this. I want you out."

"I just made a mistake."

"One too many. I can't take it anymore Mom. Look around you. Do you see what they did to my house? Our house?" Her voice shook as she fought back tears. "How am I supposed to get this mess cleaned up?" She held up her fist and shook it in her mother's face. "If I didn't love you, I'd knock your teeth out." She stepped back and let her hand fall. "I'm tired of not knowing who you're with, where you're going or where you've been. I'm tired of being a parent to you. You don't like my rules, that's fine. You need to find a place where you belong. I have to live here Mom. I have to deal with the neighbors looking at me funny because a bunch of cops tore up my place. As a child there was nothing I could do when the police busted down our door looking for drugs. It was your place, and you'd let one or more of you men use our place as a 'drop', but I will not have that here."

Rita shoved her back. "Get out of my face."

"You're not listening to me," Greta shouted, her voice raw with pain.

"All I'm hearing is you trying to sound better than me. You think you're better than everyone. You're just like my mother. You think you have the right to tell other people how to live their lives. But you don't. You're alone for a reason. No man wants you."

"And we know what men want you for."

Rita slapped her, hard. Her ring busted Greta's lip causing it to bleed.

Greta gingerly touched her lip. "Get out." She held up her

hand. "And don't say you're sorry, because I don't care right now."

Rita didn't take long to pack. She stuffed her car with her few belongings, jumped into the driver's seat and pulled out of the driveway. Greta watched her from the doorway. Her mother looked at her and gave her a crude hand gesture then drove away.

Greta wasn't offended by the gesture or the slap. She knew her mother was just angry and hurt and had to lash out at someone. She had to blame someone else for her situation and Greta had always been an easy target. She knew that in a few days, her mother would call her in tears and beg her to let her come back and Greta hoped she would be strong enough, this time, to finally say no. She'd done her mother no favors by letting her live this long without facing the consequences of her actions. Greta closed the door, then leaned against it and slid to the ground and sobbed.

"I'M sorry ma'am but that's not covered."

Greta felt like screaming at the falsely polite male voice on the other end of the phone. Although she had not been charged with drug possession, her mother's boyfriend had taken full responsibility, when it came to dealing with her insurance company they refused to pay for any of the damage, since drugs were found, and as a result, the search was justified. Although Greta could provide evidence that she was unaware that Terrell had used her house as a place to hide his stash, her insurance company would not budge. She'd spent over an hour trying to explain the situation and getting nowhere.

"Thank you," she said then hung up the phone. Greta knew that the extensive damage would be too costly for her to cover, and she didn't want to bother her grandmother. Minnie had been telling her, over and over, that one day her mother would ruin her, just like she had ruined her own life. But Greta hadn't been ready to allow her mother to be homeless.

"Greta," her grandmother had said almost as a plea. "I know you think I sound harsh, but Rita is not your responsibility."

"If not me, then who?"

"I tried my best as a mother. Your uncles turned out fine, I don't know what went wrong with your mother. But I do know this, she'll keep bringing you down. You'll regret letting her move in with you to that lovely little house you bought."

But Greta had felt confident that Rita wouldn't try her old tricks. Since moving into the three bedroom house she had bought, Rita had promised to live by Greta's rules. Marlene and Brianna were also living there, and for awhile things seemed to be working. She had no illusion that both Marlene and Rita were still using drugs, but at least they didn't bring their bad habits into the house. Finally, she felt they were safe, especially Brianna. She didn't want her niece to go through all that she had experienced. But her grandmother had been right. Her mother had filled her with regrets.

Her cell phone rang. Greta looked at the number: Vance. It was the sixth time he'd called since her return from Rhode Island and she'd ignored all his calls. She didn't want to talk to him. She didn't want to talk to anybody. She didn't want him to know about this. She was too ashamed. She turned the ringer off then put her head down on the table.

VANCE LOOKED at his phone and swore. Why wasn't she picking up? Why wouldn't she return any of his calls? He'd been short with her during their last conversation, but he didn't picture her as one to carry a grudge. Something didn't feel right. He decided that after work he'd stop by her place. He just wanted to make sure she was okay.

GRETA WAS SWEEPING up some more broken glass she found under a table, when someone rang her doorbell. She wasn't expecting anyone. She groaned imagining seeing her mother on the other side of the door. But, her mother usually hit the doorbell four to five times, just to annoy her and the bell had only rung once. Greta set her broom aside and checked the peephole. She saw Vance. He was the last person she wanted to see right now. She stepped outside and closed the door behind her.

"Hi," she said with a smile.

He didn't smile back. "I just wanted to check in with you."

She kept her hand on the door handle. "As you can see I'm fine."

"I called you several times."

Greta gripped the door handle tighter. "I know, I got your messages. I've been busy."

He glanced at the door then frowned at her. "What's wrong?"

"Nothing, I'm just very busy."

"You've been crying."

She rubbed her eye. "It's just allergies."

"And what happened to your lip?" He folded his arms. "Are you going to tell me you got stung by a bee?"

"I got stung by something," she said trying to sound flippant.

His gaze hardened. "Stop lying."

Her eyes filled with tears. "Please go. I can't deal with you or anyone right now."

Vance rested his hands on his hips. "Either you move or I move you. It's your choice."

"I don't want you to see." Greta hung her head. "I'm too tired to fight you."

"Then don't."

"Please. I don't want you to see…"

He waited.

Greta hesitated, then surrendered to the fact that he wouldn't leave. She stepped aside.

Vance grabbed the door handle then swung the door open. He stood paralyzed in the doorway.

"It was a drug bust," Greta said, answering his silent question. "Something to do with my mother's boyfriend."

"Where is she now?"

"We had a big fight and I kicked her out."

"Did she hit you too?"

"It's nothing. I just bruise easily."

He walked over to where her music stand used to be. He knelt down besides her clarinet case.

"Careful, I haven't cleaned up all the glass yet."

Vance gently lifted the case, all of the lining had been cut out and removed, the mouthpiece of the clarinet had been broken. "I'm so sorry."

The feeling in his voice let her know that he really understood what this devastation meant to her. He felt her pain. His care was too much. Greta took off her glasses and covered her eyes, wishing she could make it all disappear. Her one place of safety had been destroyed. She'd worked so hard for a place that couldn't be touched and she'd failed. "I'm so ashamed," she said in a broken whisper.

"You have nothing to be ashamed about."

She heard his footsteps come up to her and then she felt his arms around her. She started to pull away, but he just held her tighter forcing her to face her despair. She wept, the weight of her sorrow racking her body. And she cried until she felt numb and exhausted. He led her over to the couch. "I want you to sit here and let me look over the rest of the house."

Greta nodded, she was too tired to respond. Once he left the room, she rested her head back on the couch and closed her eyes. She had covered the couch with a colored sheet and substituted several brightly colored mix-matched pillows she'd bought at a flea market for the torn cushions. *Why did he have to see this?* She was glad to see him, but a part of her wished she'd been able to maintain the image she'd initially presented to him. Greta sat up and wiped her eyes and put her glasses back on. There was no use wishing. She was a practical woman and would deal with the situation. She turned when he reentered the living room looking overwhelmed.

He swore and shoved a hand in his pocket. "You know when you see this kind of stuff on TV it never looks this bad."

"I know."

He scratched his head, looked around again then sat down beside her. "Okay, what can we do?"

She looked at him, surprised by the use of the word. We? It was probably a slip of the tongue. This was her problem, not his. "I don't know. My insurance won't cover anything and this is going to be expensive. They don't cover damages related to criminal offenses, and since the police did find drugs and

Terrell, that's my mother's former boyfriend, will be facing jail time, although I was not charged, I am responsible."

Vance rested his arm around Greta's shoulders and gave her a reassuring squeeze. "Don't worry, we'll figure out something."

There was that strange word again 'we' and she liked being in his arms. He held her longer than he needed to. She didn't mind. She didn't want him to let go. Then he clapped his hands together then stood and lifted her to her feet.

"You can't stay here," he said. "Pack your things. You can stay at my place. Don't worry, I'm hardly there. I'm usually at Sylvie's."

"But—"

He gently shoved her towards her room. "Go on, I want to look around some more."

Greta was in no mood to argue. She went directly to her bedroom and quickly packed. *He was helping her. He wanted to help her.* It was an odd feeling. She was used to doing things by herself. It felt nice to have some of the weight lifted, at least for a while. She would stay at his place for a day or two, just to get her thoughts in order, and then figure out how she could fix up her place. It would take time, but she'd do it. She came into the living room and saw Vance standing in the center with a notepad.

"You're going to need a lot of work," Vance said.

"I know."

"But it's doable. Come on, let's get out of here."

Greta followed, happy to escape.

CHAPTER NINE

She shouldn't have slapped her. Rita took a long drag of her cigarette, wishing her hand would stop shaking. The shock of the impact still amazed her. Damn, she'd even drawn blood. She regretted that. Rita stubbed out her cigarette then walked into the bathroom of the motel where she was staying. She looked at herself in the mirror and scowled. She looked like crap and it was all Greta's fault. She'd had a miserable time after Greta had thrown her out. She'd gone to a couple of bars and gotten plastered and then spent the next day hugging a toilet bowl before her head stop hurting and her stomach settled.

She felt bad about the police bust. She wished Greta had just taken her at her word. Why did she always push her? She'd given her life, for God's sake, she deserved more respect. She'd carried her for nine months and popped her out after hours of agony. Making her had been a helluva lot more fun. The bitch wouldn't even be alive if it hadn't been for her. Yet she treated her like dirt. Telling her that she'd acted like the parent. She was just abnormal. She didn't understand a woman's needs. She was too much like her grandmother, dressed like her, too. She thought she was so smart, but she was just a stuck up prude.

She didn't need Greta anymore. Fortunately, she had another daughter.

HE HAD FORGOTTEN his place was a mess, but he hadn't been expecting any visitors. Vance rushed in front of Greta and picked up the jacket he'd tossed over the sofa and the different books he'd left on the coffee table. It gave him an excuse to keep busy, to maintain a distance from her. He still remembered the tears in her eyes when she'd look at her ruined clarinet case, and how good it felt holding her in his arms. He'd had to use the excuse of checking the rest of the house because he wanted to do a lot more than hold her.

"You don't have to clean up," Greta said.

"It's not the best first impression."

"You don't know mess until you let my mother stay with you a few days." She pushed an old newspaper away and sat as if she owned the place. "Relax."

He laughed. "Well make yourself at home."

She rested her arms the length of the couch. "I plan to."

Strangely, with Greta he felt most like himself. With Sylvie and his mother he always felt as if he had a role to play, but not with Greta. She accepted him as he was. She knew his past and didn't use it against him. He didn't feel as if he had to measure up to some other ideal. By showing up at his office, she'd given him a second chance. He thought he'd never see her again.

Intuitively, he knew that his true fear was that he wasn't so different than he'd once been. That Tera didn't have a reason to trust him. That he wasn't as wonderful as he'd made himself out to be. What if there was more to it? That Tera saw the real him and that wasn't good enough?

But he was, and he'd prove it. He'd show her, just as he'd wanted to in the past. She'd seen through him in the past too. He remembered one of his basketball buddies bouncing his ball off her head, knocking her glasses off. One side of the frame snapped off and they'd all laughed. He had too, because he thought he was being cool. She hadn't looked at them. She just bent down and picked up her glasses and walked away. The next day, he saw her wearing the same glasses. She had taped it together with duck tape. They'd called her the 'Gremlin'. He now knew how expensive glasses could be, and his callous behavior back then made him sick. He remembered she'd looked at him. Not at the others, and said nothing. But her disdain hit him like a fist. She knew he was a coward. She was the one who was strong. The one who was herself, no matter how others mocked her.

Vance remembered that Greta had once played a solo clarinet piece, by some obscure composer, for the school's Talent Show. She'd been booed throughout, but still finished playing the entire score. They had put her performance between a high, pulsating rap artist and a group of dancers. She'd taken her bow, in spite of the boos, and just walked off the stage. He never understood why the taunts didn't stop her. Why didn't she hide away? Their classmates, at the time, didn't know the difference between Mozart and Bad Bulldog, the popular rap artist at the time. All they knew was that one was dull and dead; the other rich. Being rich was all that mattered. Being cool was your currency. And to him, and everyone else, Greta was broke.

Vance looked at her now. She was successful in her field. So was he, but he was still hiding. Still trying to be cool. Still worried about what she and others thought. He wasn't like her. He still felt some disdain for his father. Just like Greta, he saw how others saw him. He loved his father, but it tore at him how his father was perceived. It was his father who had forced him to grow up.

They had had lots of fun having the picnic at the fountain. Greta had teased him as if they were old friends. He didn't have to forget or pretend who he used to be. And that allowed him to be who he was now. Many times he wondered who that was. He wondered if he'd somehow slip up again, which is why he felt having someone like Sylvie in his life would keep him straight. But Greta treated him as if he already had it inside him. She trusted him.

"It's a simple layout. Living room. Bedroom over there. Kitchen and Dining. Bathroom." Vance took Greta's bag and headed for the bedroom.

"Are you sure I won't be putting you out?" Greta asked as he set her bag on his King size bed.

"I told you, I rarely use it. I'm paying enough, so somebody should. I just have three rules. Don't answer the phone. Don't answer the door. And don't sleep naked."

"What?"

Vance grinned he was only half joking. The thought of her sleeping naked in his bed was too much of a distraction. "Just making sure you were paying attention."

"Are you hungry? Can I make you something?"

"What?"

"I want to do something for you. You let me cry on your shoulder and stay at your place and I want to do something for you."

Vance gripped his hands. He had to leave and he had to leave now. The more she talked the more he wanted to stay. The more he wanted her. He headed for the door. "You don't have to do anything. Just stay safe," he said, then left.

Damn he was in trouble. Vance got into his car then looked at his reflection in the rearview mirror, wishing he could feel differently. He wanted Greta and he hadn't been able to talk himself out of it. Maybe, he was being reckless again. Maybe, he was just trying to rebel because he wasn't ready to settle down yet. Maybe he was sabotaging a good thing. Sylvie was good for him. Cordell wanted to see a ring on her finger, and he didn't blame him. Sylvie wanted the same things he did. His family liked her. Greta's mother had dated a drug dealer and used to be a drug addict. He wouldn't hold that against her, but he knew his family probably would. That was, if they became serious. And they would make fun of the way she looked. There would be so much to protect her from.

Vance started the car ignition. He was a coward. That was the problem. He wanted to be with her, but he was scared. He'd lose everything. And the worst part was that he didn't even know if she felt the same way about him. Maybe if he made things more official with Sylvie the feeling would pass.

DON'T SLEEP NAKED. Greta smiled as she recalled Vance's words. She was tempted to do exactly that. To lie wrapped in his sheets completely bare. He'd never know and if he did it wouldn't matter anyway since he was just teasing her. He saw her as a friend, not as a woman, but unfortunately she could only see him as a man. An attractive, sexy man. She envied Sylvie. She envied every woman he'd been interested in. They had seen another side of him she'd never see. A man filled with desire and passion. She'd caught a glimpse of it when they were at the fountain and when he was shopping for Sylvie's ring.

But they were friends and she wouldn't jeopardize that. Just as she had felt about Drake all those years ago, she ached for his attention and kindness, but she didn't just want to be some damsel he always had to rescue. She wanted him to see her as self reliant. First she'd clean up his place. She had to have something to do. She wouldn't organize it, just freshen and tidy it up a bit. She always took pride in her surroundings and his place would be no different. Strangely, Vance's apartment didn't feel like a home. He didn't have any pictures of family or friends. It had a stark, neglected quality. She was dusting the living room when she noticed a plant shoved into the corner. She looked closer and realized it was the large potted plant she'd given him.

An acute sense of hurt pierced her. Why hadn't he kept her gift in his office? Why had he shoved it in the corner in an apartment he hardly used? Didn't he want to see it? Clearly not. She had a wild urge to throw it out and leave, the words of her mother echoing in her ears *No man wants you.* She didn't want to feel like an obligation or a duty. She'd wanted a wakeup call and she'd gotten it. She stared at the plant and uprooted the desires and feelings she'd let settle in her heart. *No matter how kind he was, she had to realize she was still on her own.*

The following day, Greta stared at the window trying to know what to do next. She'd slept on the couch, because she didn't want to get too comfortable. She'd taken a week off of work and knew she'd have to return soon and she still didn't know how she was going to fix the damage to her house. She couldn't stay at Vance's place indefinitely, and she hadn't heard from him for a couple of days, except a brief call to check in and see how she was doing.

Greta was clearing up her lunch when she heard someone open the door. She steeled herself against the joy of seeing him again. She came out of the kitchen and saw an attractive young woman come through the door. Obviously Vance's girlfriend, Sylvie. She was younger than Greta had expected, she looked barely out of college. She was model tall and thin with almond shaped eyes and skin like cocoa butter, and looked stunning in a cream silk blouse and designer jeans.

"Who are you?" she asked.

"Greta. A friend of Vance. He's just letting me stay here for a few days."

"Vance?" the young woman said, with a teasing gleam in her eye. "He lets you call him *Vance?*"

"He doesn't let me," Greta said, confused why Sylvie found the fact so amusing. "He prefers it."

"Oh I see," she said, but it was clear that she didn't.

"He's not here. Do you need to call him? Would you like me to make you something while you wait?" Greta struck her forehead. "Listen to me treating you like a guest when you probably know this place better than I do."

The young woman dropped her purse and keys on a side table and walked into the living room. "You have no idea." She inhaled. "You've been cleaning. It smells so fresh in here like lemons."

Greta shrugged. "I had nothing better to do."

The woman spun around and pointed at her. "What did you say your name was again?"

"Greta, but he likes to call me, Tera. I know he probably told you about the drug bust."

She sat down her eyes wide. "No."

Greta sat down beside the young woman and told her everything. It surprised her how much she wanted to share. She usually kept her chaotic family life a secret, but for some odd reason, being around Vance, his help and understanding, was helping her heal, and she no longer wanted to pretend about her family or her situation. "He's really been a great help."

"That's the kind of man he is. He's always been there for me. I'm just glad you're all right," she said with shock and dismay. Her gaze dropped to Greta's outfit and her eyes mirrored her sense of pity. "Did they damage your clothes too?"

"No, I grabbed what I could."

"Oh."

Greta looked down at her top and trousers. "I know, they're not the height of fashion but they work for me. So what do you do?"

"I'm a graphic designer."

"You and Vance make a handsome pair, Sylvie."

The young woman blinked, opened her mouth, then closed it and bit her lip. She jumped to her feet. "I'd better run."

"Didn't you want something?" Greta said, surprised by her sudden change.

"No, I just wanted to bug him." She grabbed her purse and keys and opened the door. "It was nice to meet you, Tera."

"You too."

Greta closed the door then kicked it. What was it about

her that made Vance and Sylvie want to get up and run? As expected, his girlfriend was just as wonderful as he was. Warm, funny, beautiful. All the men from her past had it made. Drake had Cassie. The woman she'd seen Eric with was probably perfect for him too. And Vance had Sylvie. *No wonder he'd wanted them to meet.* She had to get over him.

HE COULDN'T DO IT. Twice Vance had rehearsed asking Sylvie to marry him and imagined sliding the ring on her finger, but every time he had a chance, he froze. It had been two days since he'd seen Greta's place and he couldn't stop thinking about her. He'd stopped himself from visiting her, but that hadn't helped. Vance lay in bed and stared up at the ceiling. He couldn't pretend anymore. He couldn't pretend that he wanted to spend the rest of his life with Sylvie. He knew what his decision would mean. He'd lose his job, and Cordell's respect. But he'd coasted by most of his life. It had become a pattern. Just like getting different girlfriends to do his homework in high school, he'd allowed a woman to get him a promotion. He'd gotten all that he had around him because he planned to marry into the right family, by dating the right girl. Only a couple of months ago he felt he'd had it all and now he wasn't so sure.

Seeing all that Greta had accomplished on her own made him feel small. He didn't feel worthy. He no longer liked the man he saw in the mirror. The man who drove an expensive car and wore tailored suits. Who was he? How different was he from the boy of his past? He needed to find out. He needed to see what he was made of. He needed to find out what he could accomplish on his own. He might fail, but he had to try.

He hardly slept that night and didn't eat much the next morning. He pushed his food around on his plate. Sylvie chatted but he barely listened. He knew the words would hurt her, but he had to say them.

He put his fork down. "Sylvie I can't—"

"Shut up."

He looked at her surprised. "What?"

"Just shut up. Whatever you were about to say you'll regret it so you might as well not say it at all."

"Even though I have to?"

Her lower lip trembled. "Do you have to?"

"Yes. I can't keep doing this. I can't keep pretending—"

"That there isn't someone else?"

He released a heavy sigh. "It's not—"

"Who is she?"

"I'm not—"

"Who?" she shouted. Sylvie pushed back her chair and stood. She struck him on the shoulder. "You damn bastard, at least tell me who! Who have you been sleeping with behind my back?"

He stood, grabbing her wrist. "Sylvie—"

Tears streamed down her face. She pounded his chest. "I gave you four years of my life. I waited for you, and now you're just going to leave me? For some woman you're screwing—"

"I'm not screwing anybody," Vance said, wishing the words made it feel better. He only felt worse. He wished it were that simple. "It's not like that. I've always been faithful to you. I'm not leaving you for someone else. I don't even know if she'd have me anyway. It' just—"

Sylvie spun away and returned to her chair as if her outburst hadn't happened. "It's just a phase and it will past," she said with a careless wave of her hand. "I forgive you for having feelings, it happens."

"I can't marry you."

She held up her hands, as if blocking his words from reaching her. "And I told you to shut up. I don't want to hear it."

Vance turned and went into the bedroom. He grabbed his overnight bag and opened a drawer.

Sylvie came from behind him. She shoved it closed. "I'm not going to let you throw away what we have because of some infatuation."

He gently moved her aside and began to pack.

"I made you. You were nothing before me and my father treats you like a son. It was his connections that helped you grow the business. Don't fool yourself and think you did it all on your own."

"I know."

"You really want to give all that up because little Vanny is bored?" She grabbed his crotch and stroked him. "I know how to please you."

Vance pushed her hand away. "It's not about that."

"It usually is with you. Is she prettier than me? Younger maybe?"

He zipped up his bag. "You're every man's desire."

"Just not yours?"

He walked to the open door.

Sylvie frantically seized his arm and stopped him. "I love you, Van."

Vance shook his head and met her gaze, his heart heavy. "You don't love me. You love the man you want me to be. The man your father wants me to be. Not me."

"Don't I stroke your ego enough? Is that what she does for

you? Maybe I'm no longer an interesting challenge to you. Is she playing hard to get?"

"You're not listening to me."

"Because you're not making any sense! Of course I love you. But I should have known I couldn't keep you."

Vance briefly closed his eyes. "You're right. I can't blame you. It's me. I'm all wrong." He swallowed. "You deserve better. You deserve a man who loves you."

She pounded his back with her fist. "You rotten bastard. Don't you dare try to sound gallant."

He walked out of the room.

"Van?"

He took a deep breath then turned to her. "Yes?"

Sylvie sat on the bed and flashed a watery smile. "I feel sorry for whoever she is. You'll never be true to anyone Van. It's not your nature. The moment things get too permanent you'll bolt. Whoever she is, you're going to break her heart. One day she'll find herself in the same shoes I'm in. Losing you to someone else."

Greta had been taking a nap when a loud banging woke her. *Don't answer the door.* That had been one of Vance's rules. The pounding continued.

"Van! Answer this door. You can't hide from me. Van?"

Greta opened her mouth to tell the woman that Vance wasn't there, then decided not to.

"I know you're in there." She pounded harder. "I know what you're doing. Van! You can't treat your mother this way." She pounded again then stopped. "Okay, if that's how it's going to be. I'll talk to your father."

Greta rested her ear against the door and heard his mother's footsteps grow faint. She rushed over to her phone and dialed his number. He picked up on the first ring. "Is something wrong?"

"Your mother was here."

His tone sharpened. "You let her in?"

"No, I didn't open the door."

His tone softened. "Good."

"But she sounded really upset. She said she's going to talk to your father."

He sniffed. "Some threat."

"What's going on? What if she comes back?"

"Don't worry, I'll talk to her later. I'm still trying to figure out how to make the repairs to your house. I'll share a few options with you soon."

Greta didn't care about her house, she cared about him, but she knew she couldn't tell him how much.

CHAPTER TEN

Sylvie worked fast. Vance stared at his cell phone, amazed that his mother had already made her move. He looked around the hotel room where he was staying. He knew the fall out would be bad, but he hadn't expected it to be so swift. Unfortunately, he couldn't face Greta. At least not yet. He needed to plan his next steps. Tomorrow he'd have to finalize one major project before he handed it over to Thomas Clint, his right hand man. He knew he'd be out of a job soon. Cordell would not take Vance's breakup with his daughter well.

He had enough savings to coast for a while and he'd always wanted his own business but he hadn't planned on starting from scratch. If he presented himself to Greta now she'd probably just think of him as a loser. No, he had to get things off the ground before he made his move. He'd planned to use his connections with his present company to fix Greta's place but he couldn't do that now. He'd have to pull in some favors and spend his own money to get it done. It was not a smart business move to start in a hole, but he couldn't leave Greta's house in the mess it was.

He had to focus on what was important. He'd hand in his resignation. Look for projects he could bid on, then see what happened. He knew it would be painful. He admired Cordell. Cordell had been the father he'd really wanted. His real father was too soft hearted and weak willed, and had sent most of his money back home to family and relatives who didn't care if he lived or died. They were always sending letters, calling over the phone, or sending emails, always needing money for this and that: "Please send me some money, I need a surgery." "I'm getting married, and I need a little help" "Things are so bad, you have to send some money, now." His father's inability to say "no" had been the reason they'd lost everything. Vance didn't want to be a disappointment like his father, so he'd fight hard to build his business.

Of course his day of reckoning came sooner than he'd expected. The moment he closed his eyes to sleep his phone started to ring. First from Sylvie, then his mother, then Cordell. He ignored them all.

But Cordell wasn't a man to be ignored and the following day, he met Vance in his office while Vance tried to clear up the billing.

"I had a chat with Sylvie last night. She was in tears. You know how I feel about men who make my daughter cry."

Vance folded his arms. "I know. I didn't want this to happen, but we've grown apart and I'm not being fair to her."

"She says there's another woman."

Vance glanced down at the papers on his desk.

"My girl said you've been acting strange lately. Have you hit your head or something? Are you really going to let my daughter go so you can screw some woman who looks like a comic book character?" Cordell laughed at Vance's look of surprise. "I saw the way you looked at that woman, who came by with the large plant, and it was far from just 'friendly', although I honestly don't know what you see. You must have a nun fetish or something, because I bet she'd be about as exciting as a log in bed."

Vance gripped his pen determined not to be provoked.

Cordell sat. "The problem is you're not thinking things through. Just imagine what your parents are going to think, especially your mother. She's going to love this. And I know someone else who will love it too."

Vance set his pen down and kept his voice low. "You leave her out of this."

"Does your new lady love even know about her? No? She looks rather prim and proper. I think it will be a shock to her. I wonder what she'll think of you when she finds out."

Vance picked up his pen again. "I'll be out of your hair in a minute. I'm just—"

"I know what this is all about. You're feeling a little rebellious and want to use this poor woman to shock us. Fine. I think it's a little cruel. But I understand."

"You don't understand anything."

"If she's so special, why doesn't she know everything about you? You know I can make her life miserable. I can let her know that she's just a rebound relationship for you. We both know you've had plenty of those—you just didn't call them that. I can let her know about your one night stands and married women."

"That was in the past. A long time ago. You know I've changed and she knows it too."

"I bet you she doesn't know about—"

"That's none of your business."

Cordell flashed a cold smile. "That's where you're wrong. My daughter is my business and you're running *my* business. I own it, not you, and we had an agreement."

"Yes, my job comes with the marriage. You'll see my resignation on your desk. I just wanted to clean up a few things first."

Cordell stared at him in stunned silence.

"I'm not being rash," Vance said. "I know it seems that way, but I've thought about it."

"Look, every man hits this point. The thought of spending their whole life with one woman can be a scary prospect, so here's what I suggest. Get this woman out of your system. Keep her on the side if you like, but let's go ahead as planned."

Vance shook his head. "I can't do that."

"You're throwing away a prime opportunity."

"I know. But I like Sylvie and she deserves better."

"I invested a lot in you and you're just going to throw it back in my face?"

"I won't use Sylvie to improve my career."

"You want a second car? How about one of those homes in—"

"No. I respect you too much to use you or your daughter. I have to be fair."

"I was afraid it would get to your head. You've become too proud. What are you going to do?"

"Start my own business."

"You think it's easy to start from scratch? You think you can earn yourself a decent salary in just a year?"

"I know what it takes."

"Because I taught you everything you know. All of this." He gestured to the room. "It's because of me, not you."

"Cordell you know I respect you."

"Don't tell me that. Show me how much. Get this woman out of your system and marry Sylvie as we agreed."

"I can't."

Cordell's mouth formed into a hard line. "Fine. You don't have to finish up here." He reached over and slammed the accounting book shut. "I'll have Thomas take care of this. Just leave."

He'd expected the outcome, but that didn't make his situation any easier, Vance thought as he left the office. He'd have to call in a lot of favors to fix Greta's house. But at least now he was free to start his own business and make Greta his own. He left the building and crossed the parking lot and saw his BMW. One thing he knew for sure, was that in order to make his new life work, his prize possession would have to go.

SHE'D KILLED IT. She was a plant murderer. Greta stared at Vance's plant in dismay. Its leaves drooped and its stem looked sickly. She'd have to find a way to get him another one. He wouldn't know the difference. She'd spent a week at his place already, and he'd called and said he needed three more weeks, claiming he knew what to do about her house, but not elaborating. She'd cancelled her mail delivery and had a neighbor watch the house for her.

She'd grown comfortable at his place, so another few weeks didn't bother her. She had returned to work, although she'd missed last weeks' orchestra rehearsal and she wasn't sure when she would return. The sight of her ruined clarinet case only brought pain. She knew that she would soon hear Vance announce his engagement, and that would invite a different kind of pain, but she wouldn't think of that now. Right now she had to do something about his plant.

That Saturday, Greta went to the nursery where she'd bought the plant for Vance. She searched to see if there were others so she could make the switch. She couldn't find any. She walked up to a clerk. "Do you have any more *Phoenix roebelenii?*" That was the scientific name for Pygmy date palm.

"No, sorry. We'll get another batch next month."

"Next month?"

"Yes, they are very popular so we run out fast."

In a month Vance would see his dead plant. Maybe he wouldn't notice.

"We have to stop meeting like this," a voice said behind her.

She spun around and saw Eric. "This is a surprise."

He grinned. "Plants are my passion. Now, what's the problem?"

"How do you know there's a problem?"

"I watched you talking to that guy and then you looked as if you'd been kicked in the stomach."

Greta smiled. The description felt accurate. "I was looking for a replacement for a plant I killed."

"Are you sure it's dead?"

"It looks dead."

"Looking dead and being dead are two different things. If you show it to me—"

"I can't. It's not at my place."

"Are you house sitting?"

"Something like that."

"Okay, why don't you bring it over to my place and I'll have a look at it."

"Really?"

"Yes, really." He scribbled his address on the back of one of his business cards and gave it to her. "Come by after three today."

Greta arrived ten minutes early. She set the large plant down outside Eric's apartment, leaned against the wall and waited. She didn't want to interrupt his schedule.

The door opened and Eric peeked his head out. "I thought I heard you. What are you doing out here?"

"Waiting. You said come after three." She held up her watch. "It's not three o'clock yet."

He grinned and lifted the plant. "You're still adorable." He walked inside.

Greta followed him. "I'm not ad—" Her words fell away as she looked around his apartment in amazement. It burst with an amazing green beauty. There were several small indoor trees, exotic plants, and vines, all expertly arranged. "This is incredible."

Eric set the plant on a table he'd cleared. "Thank you and you're in luck. The plant's still breathing."

She rushed to his side. "What should I do, Doctor?"

"First tell me what happened. I think I can guess, but I want to know for sure."

"I saw it neglected in a corner so I decided to water it every day and give it lots of sunlight."

He winced. "You burned it and then drowned it." He lightly patted the side of the pot. "Poor baby." He looked at Greta. "I want you to leave it alone. Get it back in its corner and don't water it for two weeks. Once it starts to come back, then use this plant food." He grabbed a packet. "A plant can die from too much attention."

"I'll remember that."

"But I want you to play music and talk to it once in a while."

"Really?"

"It's sad. It needs positive energy. It will do you good too. Do you still play the clarinet?"

Greta hesitated. *She hadn't touched it since the drug bust.* Actually, before then, when Vance had left. "Something happened and it's been hard getting back to it."

He nodded. "You've been pouring all your energy into this plant and neglecting yourself. And now you're both withering away. Play. Plants are my passion and music is yours."

"Yes, Doctor."

"Are you seeing anyone?"

Her mouth fell open. "Why?"

"Can't a man ask?"

"A man's never asked me that before," she stuttered.

"Well one is asking you now."

"No."

"Would you like to go out sometime?"

Her mouth fell open again. "Why?"

He laughed at her expression. "Why not?"

"Because...oh I see. You mean as friends, right? I'm sorry I misunderstood you."

"No, you didn't."

"But you're seeing someone. At the restaurant you were—"

Eric shook his head. "That's over."

"And you want to go out with me?"

"If you want me to be completely honest. I want to sleep with you."

Greta blinked, then threw her head back and laughed until tears streamed down her face. *No man wants you* her mother had said. At least he'd proven her wrong. She wiped away the tears. "I think you're the only man in the world who's ever been interested."

"That's not true. I'm just bolder than most."

"Jamaican arrogance?"

"Confidence." Eric closed the distance between them and lowered his voice. "I'm older and wiser now and my technique has improved."

Greta felt her pulse quicken. "It certainly has."

"So, what do you say?"

"I can't. I used you last time."

"To get close to my brother? I know that."

She'd suspected it, but was surprised to hear him admit it. "And you didn't care?"

Eric rested a hand on his chest. "Do I look broken hearted? I can pretend to be if that will change your mind."

"No, because I'd be using you again."

His brows shot up. "You're still interested in Drake?"

"No, someone else."

"Does he know?"

"No. He's engaged. At least he soon will be."

"I don't mind being his substitute. Just don't shout out his name in the heat of passion."

Greta laughed. "You're incorrigible."

Eric's mouth twitched in amusement. "Is that a no?"

"You deserve better." She tilted her head and stared at him in wonder. "Don't you want a woman who likes you for you?"

He shrugged. "I'm not picky."

His offer was tempting. Could he be the man from her past her grandmother had hinted at? She didn't have strong feelings for him, but she did like him. If she were with him, she wouldn't think about Vance. Vance would soon be married and celebrating his honeymoon and she'd be alone again. Without Rita, her house would be completely hers. Minnie was right. She needed her own life. But when she looked at Eric it still felt wrong to use him that way. To be with him, because she was unhappy, lonely, or desperate was wrong. She wouldn't repeat her past with him. Greta playfully patted him on his cheek. "You're the one who's adorable."

"How about a kiss for old times' sake?"

Greta narrowed her eyes, and looked around the room. "Now I know what this place reminds me of. The Garden of Eden." She shot him a glance. "And you're temptation." She picked up the plant. "And I'd better go."

Eric took the plant from her. "I'll take it to your car. I swear I'll be good now."

Minutes later, he helped her settle the plant snuggly in the backseat then straightened. "Now remember what I said."

Greta got into the driver's seat. "I will."

Eric pulled out a card from his wallet. "And this is my

ophthalmologist, make an appointment when you're ready to get new glasses."

Greta glanced at her reflection in the rearview mirror. "You think I need new ones?"

"I said when you're ready and you'll know when." He kissed her lightly on the mouth. "And if you need anything, you know where to find me."

VANCE TRADED in his car for one that would fit his new life-style. Twice he'd thought of going to his apartment and talking to Greta about his plans, but he couldn't face her yet. Not until he'd gotten everything in order. He was no longer 'Van the Man', with the expensive car, the lucrative job and sexy girlfriend. Now, he was just Vance. A guy starting his own business, driving a five year old car and hoping the woman he was interested in felt the same way. He knew that Greta would accept him as a friend, but what about as a potential lover?

How would she feel about him not pulling in a regular salary until a year or two? He could bet, she made a lot more than he did. He knew getting reestablished would take time. Would she still respect him if his business took longer than expected to take off? Vance pulled up to a gas station of fill up his tank. It was too late to go back now, and he didn't want to. He felt an energy and excitement he hadn't felt in years. He was going to find out what he was made of.

He'd just finished pumping gas when his cell phone rang. Vance glanced at the number: His mother. He knew if she was this upset about him losing his job and Sylvie, she'd have an aneurism when she saw the car he was driving. He answered. "Hi."

"You've ruined everything!" she screamed. "You won't believe the conversation I just had with Cordell. How can you start your own business?"

"I'll hire Kojo." He knew that by mentioning his mother's favorite son he could allay some of her anger. His younger brother had graduated with an MBA and had yet to find a job that allowed him to use any of his acquired knowledge. He'd just been made redundant at his last three jobs and Vance knew he'd need the work.

"To do what specifically?"

"Does it matter?"

His mother hesitated. "I want so much for you. You had everything and now—"

"I'm making the choices I need to make."

"Are you sure you know what you're doing?"

No. "Yes."

"You'd better. I don't mind you ruining your life. You like to be reckless, but Kojo isn't like you."

"My battery's running low. Bye Mom." He disconnected then put his phone away.

He'd pay his brother from his savings. He knew hiring him was the only way to appease his mother and he would need someone to help supervise the men, once jobs started coming in.

As spring turned into summer, Vance got word out that he would be starting his own company. He surprised some family and friends, by deciding not to be a general contractor, but instead to limit his business to furniture restoration and conservation. He had always wanted to dive into his first love working with antiques. Growing up, he was always fixing up old pieces of furniture he'd pick up from yard sales and flea markets. He remembered his mother limiting him to their garage, telling him "I don't want you bringing that old thing in here." Then several weeks later, she would see what he'd done with a piece and take it. He loved studying the different ways furniture was made, and had taken a carpentry class at the local college.

"I hope you plan on getting a better career than cleaning up old furniture," was a constant phrase he heard from his mother. She had no idea how much could be made repairing and refinishing so called 'old junk.' Now he could put in practice what he had learned so many years before. A few years back, he had traveled to Italy, and attended a six-week apprentice program, to learn from some of the most experienced and well known furniture makers and restorers. Now he would apply what he knew. He found a space, where the rent was reasonable, and set up shop. He named his company, ML Restoration and Conservation. He decided to use the first letter of his mother and father's surnames: Minton and Lamine. Within a month, several workers from Cordell's firm came knocking.

"I can't give you the salary you need," he told them. "You have a young family to support and Clyde you're nearing retirement.

"We know that," Clyde said. "Just like you, I've put aside a small savings, I can hold on, at least for a year of two, until we get on our feet." He was an excellent worker, and experienced in structural restoration, and Vance knew that having him as part of his team would be a coup.

"I can get by." Andrew Bryson was a tall, lanky guy around thirty. "My parents said we can move in with them. They have a basement apartment I can use, until I start bringing in a salary." Vance was moved, but still not sure. He didn't mind taking the risk, but he wasn't sure he wanted others to do the same.

"We like working with you. Cordell's old school and won't try new things." By the end of his first week Vance had three full-time workers, and he was able to start work on Greta's house. Two of his best friends, one an electrician and another worked in construction, volunteered to help him fix Greta's place, donating their time. All Vance had to do was buy the material and supplies, which he got wholesale. Now he was ready to face Greta and tell her how he felt.

ERIC WAS A GENIUS. Greta looked at Vance's thriving plant with pride. She'd followed his instructions and it had turned around. She'd even played her clarinet for it, although she hadn't been able to go back to rehearsals yet, but playing again had filled her with hope. She knew that she would soon be traveling again for work and she still didn't know what to do about her house.

Greta turned from the plant and rested her briefcase down next to the couch. It had been a stressful day at work and looking at Vance's plant always lifted her spirits. It least it was one thing in her life that was working. She sat on the sofa and rested her head in her hands. She hadn't seen him in weeks and their phone calls were always cordial, but brief. Maybe he was avoiding her. Maybe he felt that he'd taken too much on by taking her in. She didn't want to be a burden. She hadn't planned on staying longer than a couple days and it had now been a couple of months.

Greta lifted her head when she heard keys in the lock. Had Sylvie come by again? Would she be the one to tell Greta that her time was up? Was she going to show off her ring? Greta jumped to her feet in surprise when she saw Vance. He looked different somehow. Tired, and the sadness she'd sensed several weeks ago was gone from his eyes, replaced by a hesitation she couldn't understand.

"What's wrong?" she asked.

"Why would anything be wrong?"

"Your face."

"I should learn to hide my emotions better. It's just been a hard week."

"Sit down. I'll make you something. It's really good to see you." Greta started to walk past him, then stopped, knowing the question that burned in her heart. "Have you asked her yet? Did she say yes?"

"Who?"

"Who else? Your girlfriend. I met her when she dropped by."

ance stared at her stunned. "Sylvie came by here?"

"Yes, I'm surprised she didn't tell you. It was awhile back. I guess it wasn't important. She was looking for you and we had a great chat."

"You did?"

"Yes, you're lucky to have each other. I can tell she really loves you."

"Sylvie came by here?" He motioned to the floor.

Great nodded. "Isn't that what I just said?"

Vance rubbed the back of his neck. She'd never done something like that before. She probably wanted to see what Greta looked like. "I don't believe it."

"She's so beautiful and kind. She told me she's a graphic designer."

His shoulders relaxed. "Oh. That's not Sylvie."

"Who is she?"

"My daughter."

"You have a daughter?"

"Yes."

"In graduate school?"

"Yes."

Vance waited for her to make the connection and silently answered her questions. Yes, his daughter was twenty-three and he was thirty-nine. He'd had her when he was sixteen. Yes, he probably should have mentioned it early. No, she didn't hear about it at school, but he didn't brag or mention it like the others did. No, he didn't keep pictures of her around, because the baby pictures he liked embarrassed her. He'd gotten in the habit of protecting himself and his daughter from the possible scorn of others for so long, he didn't know how to stop.

Some women were impressed when they learned he had a grown daughter he'd raised, with his parents help. Other, mostly those from an upper class background, thought he was quaint. But he hadn't done it as a badge of honor, but out of duty and shame. He never forgot the conversation with his father. He let him know he needed to step up to the role of being a father. Their sort didn't abdicate or skip out on their responsibility. He'd followed his father's words, but he didn't completely change his ways.

Would Greta see him in that light? As he used to be? Would she see him as the kind of guy who'd knocked up her sister? The kind of guy with smooth words and no prospects? He'd charmed his way through school, barely earning any grade he received. Getting girlfriends to cover and care for him. But that wasn't who he was now. He could have given her up for adoption. He'd kept her for selfish reasons. He thought having a kid made him a man. But he knew Greta would see through him. That's what terrified him. He couldn't charm her or seduce her or use any of his usual tricks. Why did he care so much?

"You must be so proud."

Vance blinked. She beamed at him. There was no judgment or censor. She just looked at him as if he were a proud parent, which until that moment, he'd never let himself be.

"I mean she's amazing," Greta said. "So elegant and smart."

"I'm not going to pretend that after she was born I turned my life around. It took another two years for that, but I've changed. I had to provide for her and I wanted to be a good father and role model."

"And you are. I know looking after a kid is no easy feat. You've done a great job."

"Thank you."

"Her mother—"

"Is not in our lives."

"Oh." Greta suddenly swore.

Vance laughed.

She frowned at him. "What's so funny?"

"Hearing you swear."

"You don't know everything about me."

"What are you swearing for?"

"If I'd known she was your daughter I wouldn't have told her all about the drug bust. That was not something she needed her hear. It was just that I wanted her to understand why I was there. I thought she was your girlfriend and wanted her to know everything you were doing for me, and why I was here."

"I'm glad you told her."

"Why?"

"Because I want you to know her and for her to get to know you."

"Now we do." She turned. "Let me go get you something."

Vance grabbed her arm, stopping her. "Wait."

Greta looked up at him curious. "What is it? I know something is bothering you."

He dropped his gaze. "I broke up with Sylvie."

"I'm sorry."

He looked at her, then his gaze lowered to her lips. "I hope you don't mean that."

Greta licked her lips again, her mouth suddenly feeling dry. "What?"

He took a step closer his eyes capturing hers. "I don't want you to be sorry, Tera. I want you to be glad. I had to end it with Sylvie. It wasn't an easy decision to make, but I wasn't being fair to her. I want to be with you. I can't explain why and I don't care. I like you. I like being with you. I like how you make me feel." He cupped her face in his hands then said in a hoarse whisper, "Please don't tell me I'm the only one who feels this way."

Greta shook her head.

"Good," he said then his mouth covered hers. The touch of his lips sent her senses whirling. It was dream. It was fantasy. Could she really believe this was happening? When she felt his arms circle her waist and press her close to him, she no longer cared. She wrapped her arms around his neck and kissed him back. When his hand snaked down her thigh she drew away.

"Wait, maybe we shouldn't."

He drew her close again and nuzzled her neck, his breath warm against her skin. "Do what?"

"This."

His hand inched up her blouse. "Why not?"

Greta fought to stay focused as his hand slid up her back and unhooked her bra. "You're getting over a breakup. I'm just trying to be sensible."

"I broke up months ago."

She stared at him shocked. "And you didn't tell me?"

He swung her up into his arms. "There's a lot I haven't told you."

"But where have you been staying?"

"In a hotel." He headed for his bedroom.

"Why didn't you come here?"

"I had a lot to think about. The truth is, I not only broke up with Sylvie, I lost my job too and had to trade in my car so that I could start my own business." He set her on the bed and took off her blouse. "But I don't want to talk right now."

Greta's heart pounded in her ears as her mind tried to comprehend what was happening. He'd felt this way for months? Could she believe her eyes and her ears? Her body definitely could as his hands undressed the rest of her. Her skin responding to every touch. Was this really happening? In seconds his hard body was on top of hers.

Vance's eyes searched hers with a passion that made her mouth dry and her body wet. "Are you taking anything?"

"I've never had the need too."

"You do now." He sat up. "But that's for later. Let me find something." He went to his side table and opened the drawer then he swore.

"What?"

"It's empty." He raced around the bed and checked the other drawer and swore again this time with more feeling. "I can't believe I'm out." He snapped his fingers then darted out of the room. Greta bit her lip never imaging she'd enjoy the sight of seeing a naked man run around a room. He returned with his overnight bag and frantically searched the contents. "I'm an idiot. Why didn't I take any with me? I had a whole bunch of them."

"That's not something I want to hear right now."

He had the grace to look chagrined. "Oh, right. Sorry."

"It's okay we can do it another time."

"No, I want to do it now," he said sounding like a petulant child. He upended his case, dumping the contents on the bed. "I can't believe I left one of the most important things."

"There is another option."

"What?"

"Outercourse."

"Outer-what?"

Greta lay down on her side and crooked her finger. "Come here."

Vance lay down next to her. "What?"

"Let's just touch each other."

"I don't want to just touch."

"With just our mouths." She covered one of his nipples with her mouth and sucked it then met his gaze and smiled. "What do you think?"

His reply needed no words. His mouth covered her breasts, his tongue teasing her nipples, and then making a slow steamy path up her thighs to her center, soaring her into heights of ecstasy. She returned the favor, leaving a hot trail down his stomach then lowering her mouth to the center of him, using her tongue in ways that made him gasp. She met his eyes. "You like that?"

"I dreamed about your tongue."

"My tongue?"

"Yes. When you were wetting that reed for your clarinet, I nearly lost it."

Greta giggled. "That's why you left?"

"I had to. I wanted you so bad. I still do." He kissed her, his mouth making her senses spin and soon using their mouths wasn't enough. They used their hands, exploring every inch of each other. He slid his fingers inside her, making her moan. "Next time that will be me," he whispered.

"I thought it was."

"Not the part of my anatomy I want it to be," he said with feeling. "I—"

Greta smothered the rest of his words with a kiss and quickly made him forget about condoms and anything else but her. Once satisfied, they collapsed on the bed. Greta rested her head on his chest and laughed.

"What's so funny?"

"Who would think that 'Van the Man' would end up sleeping with 'Greta the Gremlin'?"

He tenderly caressed the side of her face. "We're not those people anymore."

"No."

"I don't think we ever were."

"You were."

He shook his head. "Most of it was all show. Sometimes I felt on top of the world and others times I was scared out of my mind that I'd be found out. You scared me the most."

"I did? What do you mean by 'found out'?"

"That I wasn't who I pretended to be. But you were so confident. You didn't care what people thought."

She chuckled. "My grandmother taught me how to build a shell to protect myself. If I cared what others thought I'd never get anywhere. But I won't pretend that some of the things people said and didn't hurt sometimes."

"I'm sorry."

"Apology accepted."

"So, does that mean you'll go to the prom with me?" he

teased, taking on the bravado he'd had as a teen. "I have a lot of girls waiting for an invitation, but I'd like to take you."

"I'm not sure. That depends."

He turned on his side and looked at her. "On what?"

"Well, Drake asked me out first."

"Drake Henson? Flaky Drake?"

"Who called him that?"

"The guys on my basketball team. Of course no one ever said that to his face but the guy was just strange. He was asleep most of the time. Or always preoccupied with something."

"I liked that about him," Greta said with a dreamy smile. "He was so nice to me."

"And I wasn't."

Greta sat up, ready to put her clothes on. "No, you weren't."

Vance drew her back down on the bed, and caged her between his arms gazing at her with a steady gaze that brimmed with tenderness. "How can I make it up to you?"

Greta smiled at him, wanting him to know there were no hard feelings left. "You're doing well so far."

"So, forget the prom. How about a date? What would you like to do?"

"There's something I've always wanted to do, but you might find it silly."

"What?"

"I'd love to go bicycle riding around the Tidal Basin then we can go to that fountain near the Capitol. Oh, what's its name?"

"Court of Neptune Fountain?"

"Yes. It's beautiful, especially at night."

"Okay, let's do it."

"There's one problem."

He paused. "Don't tell me you can't ride a bicycle."

She grimaced. "I never learned how. I mean, first I never owned one, then life got busy and time slipped away and here I am."

"Fine, I'll teach you." He sat up. "Now let's get something to eat."

CHAPTER TWELVE

"I may be moving soon," Marlene said. Greta had met her sister for coffee. She tried to see her sister at least once a month and keep in touch so that she could make sure she was okay. She looked healthy and happy, even though Greta cringed when Marlene said her 'fortune teller' had told her. "She said I'll soon be going on a grand adventure."

"I'm glad to hear that."

"Mom didn't believe me."

Greta paused. "Wait, you heard from Mom?"

"Yes, she's staying with us."

"She's *staying* with you?"

"Yes, she had nowhere else to go after you threw her out."

Greta shook her head annoyed. "Again, everything's my fault."

"No," Marlene said softly. "I understand why you did it, but I couldn't just say no to her."

Greta took a sip of her coffee then picked up her biscotti. "You can't let her stay long."

"She's not too much trouble."

"She will be. She's bad news."

Marlene paused and looked down at her hands. "Sorry about what happened to your house. Mom said it was all Terrell's fault. And I know you have a right to be angry, but she's our mother."

Greta set down her biscotti, losing her appetite. "I know that more than anyone."

"People can change."

"She hasn't." Greta lowered her voice and pointed at her sister. "Remember, don't let any of her men in your apartment. Not one."

Marlene rolled her eyes. "I'm a big girl now, I know how to handle mom."

Greta wasn't so sure. Her sister was caring and her mother was manipulative. She wished she'd suspected her mother would pull something like this. Marlene was just getting her life back on track and didn't need Rita messing it up.

"You don't have to worry about us. Now you can have your own life see some guys of your own."

Greta bit her lip. "Actually I am seeing someone."

"Really? You are? What's his name?"

"Vance."

Marlene wiggled in her seat like a little girl. "I'd love to meet him."

"After the house is fixed, I'll have you over."

"I can't wait."

Greta sighed unable to shift a sense of unease. She loved her sister and didn't want her mother interfering with her progress. "If anything happens, call me."

"I always do."

"I'm proud of you. I'm proud of what you've done and I won't let Mom spoil it."

"She won't. My future is bright." Marlene grabbed Greta's hand. "You never gave up on me. You know I love you."

"Love you too."

IT TOOK Vance three minutes to know that Greta was going to hurt herself. She was a disaster on a bicycle. Greta had gone out and bought herself a bike. And, although she was determined, she couldn't keep her balance. When she fell off and landed on her face Vance rushed over to her, certain she'd want to quit. Instead, she wiped her glasses and smiled at him. "I almost got it that time, right?"

He loved her determined spirit and knew he wouldn't leave until she could ride. "Yes. You're doing great." After several tries, and bruises, Greta began to get the hang of things. She continued to improve and soon she was riding like a she'd been doing so for years. "Let's go to the Tidal Basin."

"Are you sure?"

"Yes."

They packed their bikes and headed for the perfect spot then biked around. Once again, Vance picked up a picnic-to-go from his favorite deli. After at least thirty minutes of riding, Greta indicated she needed to take a break.

They lay on the grass and looked up at the sky. "This is one of the best days of my life," Greta said. She rested on her elbow and looked at him. "Who would have thought I'd have my first time with you? I'm now just one of your many conquests."

He shook his head. "No, you conquered me first."

"I did?"

His eyes met hers. "Yes."

She stroked his chest. "I'm a woman of many talents."

He lifted her hand and kissed it. "Yes."

She smiled then looked away and her shoulders drooped.

"What is it?"

She glanced up at a bird soaring through the sky. "I'm so happy."

"And that's a bad thing?"

Her gaze fell to his face. "I'm worried about my sister. My mom is living with her right now and I don't like it, but I can't take her back."

"You don't have to."

Greta sat up and hugged her knees. "I don't know. Marlene needs support and my mother is a taker."

He stroked her back. "But your sister knows she can come to you, right? I'm sure if it gets to be too much you'll know and then we'll handle it then. What?" he asked when Greta began to grin.

She kissed his chin. "I like when you say "we"."

He bent down to kiss her mouth. "I'll say it a lot more," he breathed.

She held him back. "You haven't told me what you're going to do about my house yet."

"I've already started."

Greta widened her eyes. "You have? Why didn't you tell me?"

He grinned and quickly kissed her. "I wanted to get that reaction."

"How are you doing?"

"I'm using some friends I know and members of my own team."

"But the cost—"

He winked. "Taken care of."

She rubbed her hands together. "Can I go see?"

"It's your house. Right now, it's a mess and I've taken out some of your furniture, like your couch, to get repaired, but when we're through you won't be able to tell anything happened."

"I'll go see after work tomorrow."

They finished up their picnic, then spent the rest of the afternoon, into early evening, resting in each other's arms. They couldn't get enough of each other. As the sun began to set, they drove over to see the Court of Neptune Fountain. It was beautiful at night. It was an impressive fountain consisting of a 50-foot wide semicircular granite basin set in a retaining wall, with a set of stairs on either side. Inside the wall, there are three large niches. A 12-foot sculpture of Neptune, king of the sea sits in the middle, and on either side were images of his mythical sons.

"This is beautiful."

"I told you so. Don't you love how it's illuminated at night?"

"Very romantic."

"I used to take Brianna to a fountain where she loved throwing coins in the pool," she said feeling wistful. She had played a major role in raising her niece, but now that Brianna lived with Marlene, they hadn't been as close as before. She missed her.

"So what did you do when you threw your coins in the pool?" Vance came up behind her and snuggled her close.

"I'd make a wish."

"Did they come true?"

"All of them." *Except one.*

"Lucky girl." He said pulling her close. Greta held him close. She liked when he held her, for some reason she felt safe.

Safe from the world. Safe from her mother. Safe from her many fears.

THE NEXT DAY Greta arrived at her house and parked on the street. Several worker trucks and vans lined her driveway. She wasn't used to seeing so many people in her place. Not just people, men. But she knew she could trust them. Vance knew them and they were helping her. She introduced herself to one guy who said he was working on the electrical. Then a tall guy came up to her and introduced himself as Clyde. Dust was everywhere, and while she was sure they were doing a good job, things still looked pretty messy.

She turned down the hallway, stepping over a stack of wood planks she figured were to be used to replace the damage in her living room. She opened the door to her bedroom and saw a man inside. He quickly closed a drawer.

"What are you doing in here?"

"Nothing." He pushed past her.

But she wasn't going to let him leave until she got some answers.

ance pulled up to Greta's house, glad to see that things were on schedule. He walked past a window to get to the back door then stopped at the sound of raised voices. He looked through the window and saw Greta looking up at one of the workers who was shouting down at her. Shouting? One of his workers was shouting at a client? Let alone *his* woman? Vance gripped his hands into fists, he was about to rip out the window when he saw the man grab Greta by the arms and shove her against the wall with such force her glasses fell off.

Vance raced inside. For the first time he saw how small and vulnerable she was.

Vance grabbed the man by the neck and shoved him towards the door. "Outside."

The man stumbled towards the door. "She's crazy."

Vance went over to Greta who'd put her glasses back on. "Are you okay?"

"Yes."

"What's going on here?"

Greta kept her voice level. "He was in my bedroom, stealing."

The man pointed at her. "I wasn't. There's nothing here to steal you paranoid bitch."

Vance spun to him. "I said 'outside.'"

"But—"

Vance sent the worker a look, silently begging him to give him a reason to knock his teeth out. The man thought better of it; he turned and left.

"I'm sorry about this," he said, barely able to keep the tremor of rage out of his voice. "I'll deal with him." He left before she could say anything. He found the worker leaning against his truck. He straightened when he saw Vance. "She's just making up stories because she's a lonely woman."

"What's your name?"

"They call me RJ."

"Got ID?"

The man shook his head.

"Let me see your wallet."

"I told you—"

"Stop talking, just show me your wallet."

The man handed it over and Vance looked inside. He had no identification like a drivers license, debit card, credit card or the like. He'd have to take his word that his name was RJ. "Empty out your pockets."

RJ widened his eyes, outraged. "You believe her?"

"Now."

He threw up his hands. "I don't need this kind of grief. I quit."

Vance grabbed the collar of his shirt and shoved him against the car. "You'll quit when I say you can. Now empty out your pockets or I'll strip you naked right here and do it for you."

The man took a swing at him and Vance punched him in the gut doubling him over. He took the opportunity to dig in his pockets and pulled out a ring. He swore. He grabbed him by the face. "What's this?"

"It's my girlfriend's."

He dug further into his other pocket. "The necklace too?"

"Yea."

Vance felt sick. How could Greta trust him now when he'd introduced a thief into her home? A thief who'd assaulted her. He punched him again. And again. And again.

"Stop it!"

He turned and saw Greta staring at him in shock. He shoved the worker away. "You're finished here."

RJ turned and ran.

He could barely look at her. He held out the ring and necklace. "Here."

"Vance—"

She was going to fire him. He'd broken her trust and he didn't blame her for being disappointed with him. He knew he deserved her anger but he didn't want to hear it just yet. "Excuse me, there's something I have to do." He got into his car and drove off. He was running and he knew it. He was being a coward and he was being unfair to her. He pulled his car over to the side and parked. He shook the steering wheel and pounded it with his fist, imagining it was his brother's face and RJ's face and anything trying to force him to fail. He then took a deep breath and turned around.

∾

Greta leaned against her house and wiped away tears. She didn't blame Vance for leaving. She was bad luck. He must think she was nothing, but trouble. She hated him seeing her weak and pathetic. She rested her head against the house and closed her eyes. She wished she'd been strong enough to fight the thief. Just like the last man who'd tried to rape her sister, this man didn't fear her.

"I'm sorry."

Greta opened her eyes and stared at Vance surprised.

"If you want to press charges I understand."

"That could ruin your business. Your reputation—"

"That's not your problem."

"Yes, it is. I couldn't do that to you."

"But it's my fault. I shouldn't have let it happen."

"No, it's mine." She gestured to the two of them. "I hate this."

He reached for her. "Tera, please—"

Greta stepped back and shook her head. "No, I do." She tapped her chest. "I'm a capable woman. I'm strong. I'm smart. I had my life together. You should have seen it. I wished you'd seen me then and not now. Because now, almost every time you see me there's some sort of crisis. I'm either getting mugged and robbed or getting my house destroyed. I don't want to be a burden to you. I know how burdens can wear you down. I love my mom and my sister, but it was exhausting always looking out for her and taking care to keep my mother out of one scrape or another. Maybe the women in my family are just bad news, including me."

Vance grabbed her shoulders and searched her face. "You're wrong. You're not a burden. I *want* to take care of you and protect." He let her go and glanced away. "I'm just not doing a good job."

"You shouldn't have to take care of me."

"Why not? That's what a relationship is. You take care of me and I take care of you."

"But I haven't done anything for you."

He stared at her amazed. "You're not serious."

"Yes, I am. Okay, so I got someone to eye your car while you fixed your tire. That's it."

"I'm here because of you."

"I know. That's the problem."

Vance shook his head. "No, you don't understand. I started my own business because of you. You gave me the courage to try. You like me, just me, despite my past. I've made mistakes, but you don't hold them against me. I want you in my life as you are. Okay?" When she continued to stare at him he grinned. "This is the part where you nod and agree with me."

"I'll try."

"I'll take that." He hugged her. "Are you sure you're okay?"

"Yes."

"I know all the men who are here, so you shouldn't have any more troubles, but if you do—"

"I'll grab them by the collar, throw them out, and beat their face to a pulp like you did."

A reluctant grin touched his mouth. "I admit I lost my temper."

"That's not good for business. Next time, be a bit more civilized."

"He struck first."

"I know, but one punch would have subdued him."

"True."

"You said you were going to do something."

"Yes, talk to my brother."

His brother, Kojo had turned an extra bedroom in his house into an office. Vance wasn't ready to rent office space yet until they had enough work to cover the basic expenses. He lived there with his wife, Kara and their baby. He rang the door bell and his brother answered. "Give me a reason not to wring your neck."

"Shh..Kara's putting the baby down for a nap."

"Right now I don't care."

"Come on." He led Vance to his office and closed the door.

"I gave you the job of hiring and overseeing our temporary workers," Vance said as his brother walked to his desk.

"Yes. I did."

"I just found one assaulting and stealing from a client." Vance kept his voice low, his gaze hard.

Kojo slowly sank into his chair, his eyes wide. "What?"

"Where are you getting these workers?

"What do you mean?"

Vance struggled for patience. "His name is RJ. Who is he?"

Kojo's shoulders sagged."I was afraid of this."

"Afraid of what?"

"I was just trying to give him a chance."

Vance's voice hardened. "To do what?"

"Get back on his feet. He'd been in jail. You know how hard it is for guys like that to get work. He told me—"

"He'd been in jail?" Vance asked, flexing his fingers.

He nodded.

"For what?"

"It doesn't matter."

Vance slammed his hand on his desk. "For what?"

His brother jumped and shrunk back. "Assault with a deadly weapon."

"And you thought it was a good idea to hire him to go into a single woman's home under our seal of approval?"

"He seemed okay," Kojo said, in a small voice.

At that moment, Kara opened the door. "What's all the shouting about?"

"Your husband's an idiot."

"Vance that's not nice."

"Nice? I could get sued." He glared at Kojo. "Your problem is that you're too soft and trusting, just like Dad." He was angry at his brother, but he was also angry at himself. He should have protected her. The police bust had already violated her and he'd made her a victim again. This never would have happened with Cordell. Maybe Cordell was right. He didn't have it.

"I'm sorry."

"You think that will fix anything?"

"Stop shouting at him!" Kara said running over to Kojo and wrapping her arms around him. "What else do you expect him to do?"

The sight of Kara rushing to his brother's side enraged Vance even more. His mother did the same protective gesture. His brother was always coddled. Always taken care of and he was always the villain. The big, bad, evil older brother. He held out his hands. "You're right. This won't work. You're free of me."

Kojo jumped from his seat. "No, I don't want that. I want to work with you. Come on, Van."

Vance knew he had to give him another chance, if only because his mother wouldn't let him hear the end of it, if he fired him. He stormed out.

GRETA KNEW the moment she saw Vance that evening that the meeting with his brother hadn't gone well. He wasn't a man to hide his emotions. At first his anger with the temporary worker had frightened her a little, but she knew he'd never turn it on her.

"Want me to put some food on?" she asked.

"I'm not hungry."

He sank into a chair. "My brother and I are like oil and water. He just doesn't get it. But it's my fault. I'm the one who's too harsh. I'm the one who's too unyielding because he's perfect. He's always done the right thing. He's got a family. He's got a college degree. So, no matter what he does, he's forgiven. But me? If I chew the wrong way, it's a criminal offensive. I mean he hired a criminal, for god's sake, to work in my company. You have every right to blame me for what happened. It is my fault. I'm supposed to keep you safe."

"Look, mistakes happen."

"I can't afford those kinds of mistakes."

"You're right. So what's going to happen?"

"You saw what I did. I sent him away."

"No, to your brother."

"Nothing. Nothing ever does."

Greta reached out and touched his hand. "And that's what angers you the most, doesn't it?"

Vance nodded.

"Okay, this is what I want you to do. I want an apology."

"I can't apologize enough."

"No, I don't want your apology. Your brother needs to face the consequence of his action. You're shielding him. You're upset, but what's to stop him from doing it again? He needs to understand what his actions did to me."

Vance held her hand. "It won't work."

"At least let me try. Call him and set up an appointment for me."

"You don't need an appointment. I'll just drive you—"

Greta shook her head. "I don't want you there. It has to be between me and your brother." She held up her hand. "That's the way it has to be."

Vance sighed then picked up his phone and dialed.

THE MOMENT GRETA saw Kojo she knew he was a soft mark. He had the bright naiveté of a toddler. She knew a guy with a tender heart like him, was easy to manipulate But that trait wouldn't serve him well in business. He was tall, like his brother, but he had none of his bravado. She could see why Vance was frustrated with him. They were total opposites. Greta followed Kojo into his home office and took a seat.

"Miss Rodgers, I am so sorry about the worker at your house. I take full responsibility."

"Really?"

"Yes."

"Do you know how much that necklace means to me? My father used to beat my mother and I had to go to bed at night listening to her screams. She gave me that necklace when she died and it means the world to me."

His eyes widened. "That's awful."

"Yes, he's in prison now and I have to take care of my three younger siblings. It's been really hard getting by. I could use a break. What your brother is charging me is real steep."

"He's charging you? I thought it was at our expense."

"That's what he wants you to believe, but that's not true. I've had to sell some of my furniture just to afford the down payment."

"I'll talk to him."

Greta's tone turned flat and cold. "Why?"

He blinked. "What?"

"Why do you want to help me?"

"Because you're having financial difficulties."

"How do you know?"

He hesitated. "You just told me."

"I know what I told you, but how do you know it's true?"

Kojo opened his mouth, then closed it.

"The moment I said something you weren't sure about you should have verified. I said your brother was charging me. You thought he wasn't. What you needed to do was call Vance and find out the truth."

"I didn't want to offend you."

"You'd prefer to offend him?"

"No, I just...I don't know."

"You've been a lucky kid most of your life so you're not used to liars. You think that everybody who's hit a rough patch has just been unlucky. That's baloney. A number of them have made choices. Some use others, like you, to get what they want. You're going to hear a lot of sob stories and they're going to break your heart. Some will be real and some will be false but you're not hosting a soup kitchen. You can't afford to make stupid mistakes like the one you made. What if he'd raped me? Do you think a pathetic 'I'm sorry' would cut it after I sued your company?"

He lowered his gaze. "I'm sorry. I don't know what else to say."

"Do you want to do this job?"

He raised his eyes. "What do you mean?"

"Did you ask for this job or did your brother just give it to you?"

"We're helping each other out."

She started to smile. "You don't have to protect your brother. I know his shortcomings. He can be intimidating."

"He needed men fast and gave me the task."

"But you're not good at it, are you? You're book smart, but you can't read people and that makes you dangerous to your brother. Especially the business he's in."

"I'll learn."

"You love your brother, don't you?"

"I think he's the greatest, even though he doesn't feel the same."

"He cares about you."

"Only because our mother forces him to. I wish I could be like him."

"You don't have to be."

"I want to make this work. I want to make him proud. But he thinks I'm weak like our father."

"Your father?"

"Yes, because he was always so generous, a little too much so. We had a lot of financial troubles growing up. Once we nearly lost everything and had to live in a dive in a rough part of D.C. We didn't know where our next meal would come from. Mom almost divorced him, she couldn't take it anymore. We finally recovered, but Vance never forgave him."

"I'm sure your father's a good man and you are too. You just need to use your strengths." She looked around his office. "You're good with organization."

"I like things to be in their place."

"I think that's how you can help your brother. Tell him—"

"*Tell* him?"

"Yes, tell him what you're willing to do. You have to stand up to him."

Kojo shook his head. "That's harder than you think."

Greta knew he was right. They needed a neutral ground that Vance couldn't dominate. She started to smile as an idea came to her. "Let me make it easy for you. How do you feel about soccer?"

CHAPTER FOURTEEN

He should have gone with her. Vance checked his phone a fifth time. Still no update. What did she think she could accomplish? He had to trust her. He heard the keys in the lock and then Crystal, his daughter entered.

"Hi, Dad."

"How many times have I told you to knock first?"

"You gave me the keys for a reason."

"Yes, in case of an emergency."

She kissed him on the cheek. "I'll remember next time. It's been hard to reach you these last couple of months."

"I've been busy."

"Grandma's still recovering from your breakup with Sylvie."

I don't care. He checked his phone again.

"You're in a grumpy mood."

"Hmm."

"We need to talk."

"You know I hate when a woman says that." He pointed to a seat. "What's on your mind?"

She crossed her legs. "I met Tera. I mean really?"

"Really what?"

"Didn't you hear me? I just said I met Tera."

"Yes, she told me," he said absently. He didn't want to talk about Greta. He wanted to hear from her.

"Grandma thinks she's a joke. Some weird phase you're going through. Is she, right?"

Vance gritted his teeth. "What do you think?"

"I think Tera's sweet, but she needs to work on her appearance, judging from her hairstyle and clothes. And those awful glasses definitely have to go."

"I didn't mean what do you think about Tera," he said keeping his voice level. He didn't care what anybody else thought about Tera, not even his daughter. "I mean, do you think I'm going through a phase?" He waved his hand when she opened her mouth. "And it was a rhetorical question because it isn't a phase and I like her the way she is."

"Why didn't you tell Tera about me?"

"I didn't want her asking questions." He rubbed his chin. "I thought I'd be over her before you knew about us."

"Why do you let her call you Vance?"

"Because I don't want to remind her of my old nickname in high school."

"I'm sure it doesn't matter now."

His daughter was biased and loved him unconditionally. No woman looked at him with the love and devotion he saw in her eyes. Probably because he never inspired such feelings in them. He never cared. His daughter was the only person he really trusted. The only one he let into his heart. He'd used her to keep woman away, and now that she was grown he couldn't use that excuse anymore. Perhaps his daughter was right.

Greta didn't fit the image of the woman he was usually with. He thought it would bother him, but it didn't.

His cell phone rang. Vance snatched it and checked the number: Greta. "How did it go?"

"Are you busy?"

He looked at his daughter. "Am I busy?"

She shook her head.

"No. How did it go?"

"Fine. I'll tell you when you get here. I found a place you'll love. It's an out of the way bar that has a big screen that shows international soccer matches." Vance couldn't imagine such a place. He thought he knew all the places to go to watch a soccer match.

He sat up. "You did?"

"Yes, I'm sending you the directions. See you there." She hung up.

"She's amazing."

"What's going on?" Crystal asked, curious.

"Tera found a place that sounds like heaven." He grabbed his coat then frowned when she did the same. "Where are you going?"

"I'm coming with you. If this is the real thing, I don't want to miss anything."

IT WAS THE REAL THING. It was a wonderful noisy, colorful, 'jumping' restaurant with a great bar and several enormous flat screen TV's. Although a game was playing on the screen, the deep beat of music could still be heard. Vance spotted Greta waving at them from across the room and he made his way over to where she was sitting. He kissed her and then formally introduced her to Crystal. He looked around amazed. "How did you find this place?"

"My secret. I ordered some jerk chicken wings and beer, I hope you don't mind."

"Sounds great. How did the meeting go with Kojo?"

"You're about to find out." She waved at someone near the door. Vance turned and saw his brother.

"What's he doing here?"

Greta stood. "He needs to talk to you."

"Wait, where are you going?"

"I have to go to orchestra practice." She kissed him on the cheek. "Now, enjoy the food and the game, and remember to listen."

Kojo gave his niece a hug and kiss, then took a seat next to Vance.

Vance folded his arms. "So you have something to say to me?"

Kojo swallowed. "I want to be put in charge of dealing with the finances and the paperwork related to all the jobs."

"But I need someone who can deal with hiring and overseeing the workers, especially the temps"

"That's not me."

"But—"

"Van, I really want to work with you and I'm great with organization, administrative and legal matters. Hiring and working with people just isn't my thing."

"Obviously."

"Dad, just listen," Crystal said.

"I am listening."

"You know I'm good for it. I wouldn't say I wanted to do something if I didn't mean it. I know my work history is spotty, but I think this is me and I want a chance to do what I know I'll be good at.

"I'll think about it."

Kojo nodded then looked around. "This is an amazing place. Remember when Dad used to take us to matches?"

"Yes." Vance answered, sadly. He remembered how no matter how bad the weather was, if there was a soccer game in town, his father, Kojo and Vance would be there. Their father loved soccer. He had been an excellent player, back home in Ghana, and had even been recruited to join a professional soccer team, but his father, their grandfather, hadn't approved. He wanted him to go to university instead. Which he did, specializing in sports' medicine. When he came to the U.S. he used his knowledge to partner with a fellow Ghanaian and opened a successful sports clinic, making an astounding amount of money for his family until poor decisions got in the way. Namely, he could not say "no" to anyone. Vance looked at his brother and knew the courage it had taken him to tell the truth. Kojo was right. He wasn't good with people and Vance shouldn't try to make him. He'd talk more with him later. Right now, he didn't want to discuss business, he just wanted to enjoy himself.

Vance watched the game while they ate some of the best home-made fries and deep-fried onion rings, while engaging with his brother and soon, with some of the other patrons. Every now and then, everyone was shouting at the screen and cheering at the scores. The game was between Nigeria and Spain. For the first time, in a long time, Vance felt relaxed and happy. Crystal watched him, intrigued. She stared amazed when her father gave her uncle a friendly slap on the back. She'd never seen her father so carefree.

Even the way he looked at Tera surprised her. While

others gave them a curious glance her father didn't care. That wasn't like him. He usually was very aware of how he was perceived. Image was everything. At least it had been before Tera. He didn't talk about soccer because it wasn't a popular American sport. He only dated woman who were eye candy. Tera had made her dad happy but Crystal knew she would never get past her grandmother. Greta would need to do something about her looks. Crystal thought about her plan as she and her father returned to his place.

"Dad I need some money."

"What for?"

"I want to do something nice for Tera."

"Like what?"

"It's surprise."

He fell silent then asked, "How much do you need?"

"Five hundred."

"Try again."

"Isn't she worth that much?"

"Try again."

"Are you strapped because you lost your job?"

"You have a job," he countered. "Why are you asking me for money?"

"Okay. Two hundred. "

"Fine."

THAT NIGHT VANCE entered his apartment surprised to find all the lights out. Had Greta returned from practice and gone to bed? He cautiously opened the bedroom door then stopped when he saw it was empty. Where was she? Had something happened? He grabbed his phone and called her. His heart returned to his normal pace when she picked up.

"Hi?"

"Where are you?"

"At home. Did you have a good time?"

"What do you mean?" He said turning on all the lights. "Where are you?"

"At home. My home."

He stopped. He'd gotten so used to her being at his place. He'd started to think of it as her home too. "Why?"

"I have to travel and I have a lot of my things here." He'd been on the site earlier that day, and things were still pretty rough. A lot of progress had been made, but the repairs were not complete.

"Oh," he said, not knowing why he suddenly felt lost. He'd wanted to be with her tonight. "When do you leave?"

"In two days."

She didn't offer to invite him over and he didn't want to push her. "I'll miss you."

"I promise to send you pictures of fountains."

He didn't want pictures of fountains. He didn't want to talk to her over the phone. He wanted to come home and find her there. Or, know that she'd be coming home to him. He didn't realize how disappointing the thought was of going to bed alone. It had never bothered him before. He'd slept apart from Sylvie a number of times. But after his great experience at the bar and talking to his brother all he could think of was being with her and asking her how her rehearsal had gone. She had told him that her orchestra was preparing for an upcoming performance. He also wanted to ask her what she'd said to his brother to make him finally stand up for himself. Something felt wrong. Had the incident with the thief made her want to distance herself from him?

"Vance are you still there?"

"Can you come by tomorrow?"

"I'm afraid not."

"So I can't see you before you leave?"

"I'll see you when I get back."

He sighed. "What did I do wrong?"

"Wrong?"

"Tera, a man knows when he's in the doghouse."

"Doghouse? What are you talking about?"

"Since the incident with that thief we haven't been together. You went to my brother alone and then left me at the bar and now I come home and you're not here and you're telling me you're traveling and I'll see you when you get back."

"And I mean it. I'm not holding anything against you about what happened. I told you why I wanted to meet with your brother and I thought it would be best that I wasn't there when you two spoke. I came home because I have to travel and I have a lot to do. That's all. I'd like to see you, but I can't. Really."

He'd have to believe her. He didn't want to sound possessive, although he felt that way. "Okay."

"You'll look after my house for me?"

"Of course. This time when you come back you'll have a great surprise."

"I look forward to it. Bye."

"Bye."

Vance hung up the phone then sat on his couch. The place felt empty without her. He'd gotten used to her tidying up and working on her laptop. He sighed. He'd never felt this way before. He enjoyed having his space. Sylvie had always talked about them moving in together, but he'd balked at the idea.

Now he wondered. What would Greta think of the idea of moving in with him or him moving in with her?

GRETA STARED at her phone wondering if she'd handled Vance well. He had sounded upset, but she couldn't understand why. Why would he think he was in the doghouse? Why didn't he know she'd forgiven him for the incident with the thief? He was right though. She had tried to not be alone with him. Had he somehow sensed that she'd lied to him? That she was keeping things from him? She hadn't gone to practice that evening and she wasn't sure if she'd ever go back. She couldn't focus the way she could before. She couldn't see Joan and pretend that her life hadn't faced a major upheaval.

It was hard being back at her place with it still in chaos, but she had to face the reality of her life, not hide from it. But she didn't want to be a burden. She still felt guilty about the situation at her house. Even though she knew the raid hadn't been her fault, she didn't want Vance to think he would always have to get her out of scrapes.

She used to be a woman she was proud of. A confidant, woman who was a member of an orchestra, went to rehearsals, practiced her clarinet nearly every day, or at least tried to, and frequently traveled for her job. A woman who had her life in order. She had to show Vance that she was independent and resourceful.

CRYSTAL SEARCHED through the racks of a local consignment store hoping to find the right outfit Tera might like. She hadn't been able to squeeze more than $200.00 from her father, he had a habit of being stingy – money-wise, but she understood. He had just started his new business, and things would be tight for awhile. So, she had decided to add $200.00 from her savings.

"How long are you going to take?" her boyfriend grumbled.

"I didn't ask you to come with me."

"I know, but you know I like being with you."

Crystal held up a jacket. "Do you like this color?"

"It's too old for you."

"It's not for me. It's for my Dad's girlfriend."

"She can't get her own clothes?"

"It's a gift."

He pointed to another rack. "How about that black one over there?"

"Oh yes, that would be nice."

"Good, can we go now?"

"No, now I need to get her some accessories."

HE WAS GOING to be cutting it close financially. He'd been overly optimistic about the number of clients he'd been able to get, but their projects weren't big enough. Vance looked at the pattern he'd carved into a table leg. When completed the table would be a beauty but he'd need a lot more commissions like this to make a profit. Maybe Sylvie and Cordell had been right. The success of the CA Construction had nothing to do with him. He didn't want to let his men down. Although they had faith in him a number of the former clients he'd worked with, didn't. At least Greta's house was done now and he couldn't wait for her to see it.

"Quite a little workshop you have here," Cordell said walking in the door.

Vance glanced up stunned. Cordell was the last person he expected to see. Part of him was glad to see him. He admired Cordell and didn't want any hard feelings between them. "Nice to see you."

"Business is booming over on my side of town and I thought I'd come over here and see how things are going."

Bad. "Fine." Vance picked up his carving tool.

"Sylvie's seeing an architect. Son of an old friend of mine."

"I'm happy for her," Vance said his mood dimming as he realized why Cordell had come. He'd come to gloat. To say "I told you so". It stung to know that a man he'd admired for so many years, a man he'd seen as a father-figure, took delight in seeing him struggle. It was clear that the respect and admiration had been one-sided.

"I bet you thought stealing some of my men would have helped you," Cordell said with a smirk.

Vance adjusted the clamp holding the back of the table leg and returned to carving. "They came on their own."

"And I bet they're already having regrets."

Vance made a quick movement with the carving tool, missing the wood and slicing through his hand. Bright blood gushed out. He swore and grabbed a rag nearby and wrapped it tightly around his hand.

Cordell came over to him, handing him another rag.

Vance pushed past him. "You won okay? I get the message." He scrambled for his car keys, blood seeping through the rag and staining his shirt.

"At least let me drive you to the hospital."

"No, and I don't want to see you when I get back." Vance closed up shop and jumped in his car. His hand hurt like hell, but what he hated more was doing something so stupid in front of Cordell. He'd been angry. But more at himself. Cordell had touched on all his fears. That he wasn't good enough or smart enough. Would Greta eventually think so too? He'd hated school and she'd gotten a bunch of degrees. He'd knocked up a girl at sixteen and it had only been luck that he hadn't knocked up others, before he got his act together. Greta had always been responsible. More than once he'd wondered if his feelings for her were stronger than her feelings for him. He wouldn't be surprised.

He pulled over to the side of the road. His vision was getting blurry and he couldn't focus. He couldn't understand why, he didn't think he'd lost that much blood. But he wasn't himself. He picked up his phone and dialed.

"Hello?" a deep voice said.

Vance took a deep breath then said the words he never thought he'd say. "Dad? I need your help."

CHAPTER FIFTEEN

Greta got off the plane after a long trip, ready for a hot soak and then a nap. She grabbed her luggage from the airport luggage carousel on the lower level.

"Tera!"

She turned and saw Crystal rushing over to her.

"Sorry I'm late. I looked for the wrong flight and then when I figured out the right one, you'd already come here." Greta was somewhat stunned. She hadn't expected anyone to come and pick her up. How did Crystal know when she was coming home? Ah, Vance.

"Crystal what are you doing here?"

"I wanted to see you before you saw Dad. You're going to see him today, right?"

"Actually I was going to go straight home and—"

Crystal continued as if Greta hadn't spoken. "But I thought it would be great if you gave him a surprise."

"A surprise?"

"Yes, I have everything in this bag." She lifted the large shopping bag up. "You'll look great."

Greta frowned. "What are you talking about?"

"A makeover. You know my dad's a good looking guy and he has a certain image to maintain," Crystal stumbled over her words, as if unsure how to frame them. "He likes his ladies to have a certain image too."

Greta started to grin. "Has he had a lot of ladies?"

"Yes...I mean no...I mean."

Greta's grin widened. "It's okay. It doesn't matter."

"What I'm trying to say it that I'm here to help you."

"Help me?"

"Yes, with a makeover. I don't want to be mean, but your clothes are a little old fashioned and your glasses are *way* too big for your face." When Greta didn't appear offended, Crystal continued. "You know, as a graphic designer, I see everything as a visual display...what I'm trying to say is I bought some items I thought you'd like and makeup and... Hold on." She reached into the bag and pulled out a sequined multi-colored skirt wrapped in tissue paper. "Isn't this gorgeous?"

"How much did you spend?"

"I squeezed some money out of Dad," she said with a proud grin. "And I used some of my own."

Greta looked dismayed. "You didn't have to do that."

"I wanted to."

Greta took the skirt from Crystal, held it up, then refolded it. "This is very kind of you and I know you've put a lot of thought into it but I can't accept it."

Crystal's face fell. "Why not?"

"It's just not appropriate. I don't feel comfortable with you trying to dress me. But here's what I'll do," she quickly added when Crystal's eyes filled with tears. "Tell me how much everything totaled and I'll pay you back. Okay?"

Crystal sniffed and nodded.

"Perhaps another time we can go shopping together," Greta said, even though she hated shopping.

Crystal flashed a watery smile. "I'd like that."

AN HOUR later Greta sat in her grandmother's sitting room, telling her about her meeting with Crystal at the airport. She'd been so steamed by the encounter she hadn't been able to go home. She had to vent to someone she knew would understand. "And then she gave me this," Greta showed her grandmother the skirt. "I felt so embarrassed that she feels she needs to buy me clothes so that I can be good enough, excuse me, have the right 'image' for her father."

"Poor thing. Her heart was in the right place."

"I know. I nearly made the poor kid cry, but I don't like feeling like a charity case. I'm donating the clothes. Vance already feels he needs to help and rescue me and now his daughter does too."

"It's what people who care about each other do."

"Maybe she has a point. We do make an odd pair. I'm not blind, I know that. Maybe he feels responsible for me for some awful reason. Maybe, he just feels sorry for me."

"Greta, from everything you've told me about him, it's clear he has feelings for you."

"Part pity, part—"

"You're being unfair. Are you afraid to trust him?"

A little. His daughter's words had wounded her pride. "Maybe we should just be friends. I don't want to have to change to be with him."

"You don't have to change."

"But she wants me to. Maybe I am blind or something. I thought he liked me just the way I am. He's never mentioned, or even hinted that I should change the way I look. But, maybe he shared his concerns with his daughter. Maybe he's using his daughter to let me know that he wished—"

"Sister, stop right there. You are just making up stories. Just take what she did for what it is. She wants you to improve what you have. I do too. It's not the first time we've had talks about how you look. You like to stay hidden behind your lab coat, and since you work with those nerdy scientists, you never take the time to work on and enjoy your outer, as well as inner, beauty. I want you to be who you are, but I'm sure he wouldn't mind seeing you clean up a bit."

"This is who I am."

"When was the last time you went to an ophthalmologist or the beauty salon?"

Greta thought about Eric giving her a card for his optician. She groaned. "Even he wanted me to change."

"Who?"

"Never mind. I just haven't had time for those things."

"Well now's the time. You're venturing into a new life. One without your mother, sister or niece, and you need a new look to go with it. The problem is you're scared."

"I'm not scared. Okay a little scared. What if I get all dressed up and it's still not enough?"

"Don't worry, it will be."

"You haven't met his daughter."

"No, and I haven't even met him yet. Why is that?"

Greta shrugged. "The right moment hasn't come up yet."

"Does he mean a lot to you?"

"Yes."

"Then prove it. It may seem silly, but men are visual creatures. I'm not asking you to change yourself. Spruce up a bit, and stop wasting the good genes I gave you. Remember if you want a good 'catch' you have to put out a line."

It sounded so simple, but Greta didn't want to admit to Minnie, that she didn't know how.

VANCE LEFT the hospital with stitches, a swollen hand and plenty of pain pills. He wasn't in any pain, but he felt like an idiot. His father had picked him up and his brother and sister-in-law had dropped his car at his place. His father hadn't said much on the trip to the hospital or on the way to his house and he was glad. He didn't want any questions or a conversation that fell into recrimination.

He sat and gazed out the car window then stiffened when he saw the time and date on a bank sign. Greta was arriving back today. He'd wanted to be waiting at her house with flowers but he was too tired to even move. She'd see the changes to her house without him. The day just kept getting worse. He swore.

His father looked at him. "Are you in pain?"

"No, I just...It's nothing."

"You know the first few years of a business can be hard. Some people take off like a rocket, others putter along. The key is to persevere."

"Hmm." Throughout his life his father was always offering him advice he'd chosen to ignore. But this time, he felt like listening. "Why aren't you angry with me?"

"Angry?"

"Yes. I know I disappointed Mom when I left Sylvie and my job and—"

"Your mother wasn't disappointed, she was just scared for you."

Vance couldn't imagine his mother being afraid of anything. She'd always done what she wanted.

Bernice Minton was a proud woman from the south who'd come up north to study to be a nurse. She had met Kwame Lamine at Georgetown University hospital where she was a nurse and he a second year resident. She had fallen for the handsome, soft spoken Ghanaian who spoke of a large family that rivaled hers. She was used to large family gatherings and people being in other people's business, so marrying someone with a large family didn't intimidate her. After a year of dating they decided to get married, and he took her home, briefly, to meet his family.

That's when the trouble began. "I've taken lots of risks in my life, so I understand her fear," he continued. "I took on more than I should have. I had a successful business and thought I could help the world. But before long I began to drown, I found myself trying to support my family in addition to sending money home to take care of my aging mother, father and ten siblings. I was the eldest son, and by tradition, I was responsible for taking care of them."

"But you didn't just take care of your immediate family," Vance said, with remembered bitterness. "You helped others at the expense of us."

"Yes," he admitted with a tired sigh. "I also felt responsible for aunts and uncles and even my cousins. The stories they'd tell me of how bad things were and how blessed we were, I felt it was my duty to help them. But I didn't love you less. I'm sorry if you ever felt that way."

All Vance remembered was how he resented his father's divided loyalties. How his father's generosity had led to him losing the Sports clinic, then finding themselves living off their mother's paycheck, which at the time could barely pay for their food and bills. He could understand his mother not wanting that kind of life for him.

"I can understand Mom being scared. I'm scared too," Vance admitted ready to hear his father's disapproval.

But it didn't come. Instead his father grinned. "Good. That'll keep you sharp, but that should never stop you."

He nodded, letting his father's words sink in then returned his gaze to the window surprised that he felt more empowered than before. All the respect he'd wanted from Cordell his father had for him all along. Despite all his mistakes, all his anger, his father's love had never wavered. . He realized that most of his life he'd wanted another father, when he'd had the one he needed all along.

GRETA STOOD TRANSFIXED in the doorway and stared at the inside of her house in awe. At first she'd approached her house with some trepidation, but then gathered her courage and opened the door. Everything was back in place and no one would be able to tell what had happened. Her grandmother's couch looked perfect.

She called Vance eager to thank him, but both his home and cell phone went to voicemail.

Her doorbell rang.

Greta ran to answer the door expecting to see Vance, but Joan stood there instead.

"Where have you been?" she demanded. "You haven't been to practice for ages and I got worried."

Greta opened the door wider for her to enter. "I know. I had a family emergency."

Joan stepped inside then gasped.

Greta spun around to see what was wrong.

Joan gripped her chest. "Your home is exquisite. From the outside you'd never be able to tell. Oh my goodness. Look at the woodwork. Do you mind if I look around?"

Greta smiled feeling a little stupid. "No," she said. And it was through Joan's eyes and description that she really saw what Vance had done. He had hired a skilled carpenter to replace all of the original wood trim, exactly like it was new. Polished bamboo floor planks gave the entire house a sense of sophistication, and all of the damaged wood paneling had been replaced with mahogany. The doors to her kitchen cabinets had been replaced with a sleek set of white laminate doors with finished antique brass handles.

A lot of attention had been paid to getting the basement back in shape and her favorite place, the back porch. As part of the restoration in the porch, Vance had installed new floor-to-ceiling windows and two skylights. A view of her back garden could be seen from every angle, and the openness of the floor plan allowed the sun to shine through brightly year-round. And as a special treat to her, Vance had taken the time to restore her grandmother's couch, including the carved wooden claw feet, and the upholstery had also been matched to the original print. He had ordered the fabric from a specialty store in Italy. Greta could hardly believe it was the same house. It was breathtakingly beautiful.

"I'm so jealous," Joan said returning to the living room and taking a seat. "Who did you use?"

"My boyfriend."

Her eyes sparkled with mischief. "The contractor? I knew

you were more than just friends. I guess it doesn't matter if he isn't too bright if he can do this."

"He focuses on woodworking and restoration now, and he's very clever."

"I don't care, honey. If he can do this I want his number."

Greta gave Joan Vance's information then the two chatted for a while. Then Greta slowly got a new resolve. Vance had done all this for her and now she wanted to do something for him. "Who does your hair?" she asked Joan. When Joan just stared at her, she hurried to explain. "You always look so finished and—"

Joan clasped her hands together as if she'd just been offered a grand prize. "You want to get your hair done? I know someone you'll love." She then shared horror stories of stylists who cut her hair either too short, or gave the wrong color. "But he is amazing. I'll make an appointment for you."

Greta opened her mouth to protest then stopped, she had to get used to people wanting to help her. "Thank you."

"Not a problem. Now, how do you feel about makeup?" They talked some more and then Joan left. Greta tried Vance's number again. No response. When she tried again the next day she started to get worried. *Don't worry about me,* she could hear him say, but she couldn't help herself. After work she drove to his place and knocked. It took him a while to answer and when he did he looked awful. His face looked drawn, his eyes were barely opened and his left hand was bandaged.

"Greta," he said bending forward and giving her a clumsy hug. "You're back."

"I've been back for a while," she said stumbling back from the weight of him. "What happened to your hand?"

He ambled over to the couch, then collapsed into it as if he had no energy left. "I was stupid. I had an accident at work."

He yawned. "And these damn pain pills keep knocking me out. I can hardly keep my eyes open."

"You can get another prescription."

"Hmm." He rested his head back and closed his eyes. Greta assumed he'd fallen asleep until he said, "I'm so glad to see you." His eyes remained closed his breathing was labored as if he was using all his energy just to stay awake.

"Go to sleep."

He looked at her through half closed eyes. "I don't want to."

She smiled, it was a losing battle. "You need to." She kissed him on the cheek. "The house looks wonderful."

"I wish I could have been there."

She rested her head on his shoulder. "Me too."

CHAPTER SIXTEEN

*A*fter putting Vance to bed and making sure he had all that he needed, Greta returned home and for the next two days watched several makeover shows. She took some notes and also went to her local bookstore and picked up a book on how to change one's appearance. By the end of the week, she felt a little overwhelmed, but decided to take things one step at a time. After visiting Joan's hairstylist in D.C. where she had a new haircut and color added, she made an appointment with a makeup artist at one of the major upscale department stores.

Once again, she was hesitant, and interviewed several before she selected the person she wanted to work with. And she wasn't disappointed. Instead of making her up to look like some painted clown, the makeup artist asked her questions about what she did, the colors she liked and what kind of look she wanted to achieve. Greta spent at least two hours getting made over, and purchased close to half a paycheck worth of makeup and perfume. She didn't mind, she hadn't done anything like this for herself. She was always busy spending her money and buying for others.

Next Greta made an appointment at a small boutique she had found listed in the yellow pages. It was the perfect place for her. The owner, a former fashion model, spent an entire day with her selecting a number of items and ensembles that fit Greta perfectly. Nothing was ignored. In addition to a couple of fitted blouses, Greta bought several skirts, five designer dresses, seven tailored pants, a couple of casual jeans and one leather and linen jacket. By the time she left, she felt like she was on top of the world. The following day, she went shoe shopping. It was not an experience she would say she enjoyed. She had large wide feet, and she didn't like wearing high heels. Thankfully, after visiting a number of stores with no luck, she happened upon a no-name shoe store, where the owner helped her select several attractive, but sensible shoes, in addition to several low-to-mid-heels, for special occasions.

Her wardrobe was looking just the way she wanted. She loved how her new haircut and coloring made her look and feel, but she knew she was missing some important items. When she'd watched one makeover show, she noticed how important wearing the proper lingerie was. She decided to visit Divine Notions, a lingerie store she'd spotted near downtown.

"What are you looking for?" a tall, svelte black woman asked her. Her long purple black hair fell to her shoulders in big curls. She was beautiful and sexy. Greta froze, feeling like a mule among stallions.

"I don't know," she finally managed.

The woman smiled. "That's fine. My name is Adriana Travers."

"Greta."

"Is this your first visit to a store like this, Greta?"

Obviously. She knew Adriana was just being polite. She nodded. "I'd like to impress my um...friend."

"Serious or casual?"

"Uh—"

Adriana winked. "I'm just teasing you. It doesn't matter. What does he like?"

"I have no idea. Should I have asked him first?"

Adriana laughed. "No, I don't mean in terms of lingerie. I mean what are his interests?"

"Oh. Um...he's a basic guy. He likes soccer and...oh yes. he loves fountains."

Adriana walked to a display on the far wall. "Okay, then I think you'll like this..."

VANCE FINISHED his beer and ordered another one, feeling restless. He knew Greta was back in town, but he hadn't been able to see her since she'd stopped by. He could hardly remember it. He'd stopped taking the pain medicine the next day. He wanted to see her again, but she said he'd have to wait for the weekend. At least business was picking up, he'd gotten a call from a woman with an interesting and lucrative request, plus his relationship with his brother had improved. He looked over at Kojo who was discussing a soccer play with another patron. They'd made it a weekly tradition to meet at the sports bar for drinks and to watch a game. Vance enjoyed it more than he'd expected and wondered if he should invite his father to come along.

He thanked the waiter for the beer and was about to drink it when he felt the energy in the room change. The moment he glanced at the door he knew why. A gorgeous black woman, wearing a short jacket with the collar up, and a pair of killer three-inch heels had entered. She had a curvy, regal figure that could leave a man speechless.

She glanced around the room and then their eyes locked and a slow sensuous smile spread on her lips. He felt an instant attraction and swore. He tore his gaze away. He was off the market. He was with Greta now. He wasn't the man he used to be. If he'd been younger, he would have imagined her naked then calculated how long it would take to make that a reality. He took a long swallow of his drink, to cool his insides.

"Is this seat taken?" she asked, sliding into the seat, as if the answer didn't matter.

"It is now," he mumbled. Vance glanced up at his brother. Kojo stared at the woman like a prepubescent boy in awe. He kicked him under the table. Kojo blinked several times, as if coming out of a trance and cleared his throat.

Vance lifted his glass, determined to focus on the game.

The woman reached over and stroked his back and leaned toward him, her perfume invading his senses. "You look tired, is everything okay? How's your hand?"

Vance jerked away from her, surprised by her boldness, but not surprised by how his body responded. Her touch was like an electric charge shooting through him. And why was she acting so worried about him? Just like Greta. He paused. Even her voice sounded like Greta. He slowly turned and met the woman's beautiful brown eyes. They were no longer hidden behind glasses.

"What's wrong?" she asked.

He shook his head unable to form any words.

"You look amazing," Kojo said. "He didn't recognize you."

Vance kicked him hard enough to make him wince.

Greta smiled. "Do you like what you see?" She playfully tugged on her skirt.

He nodded.

"Good." She leaned forward and whispered. "I hope you'll like what you presently don't see too." She stood. "But let me go get a drink." She left the table before he could stop her.

He saw the men watch her walk over to the bar.

"She doesn't even know how beautiful she is," Kojo said.

Vance gripped his glass. Tonight he planned to show her.

GRETA PLACED her order with the bartender feeling like a queen. Vance was so easy to please. If a new hairstyle, some lipstick and contacts could put an expression like that on his face, it was worth the effort. She had decided to ditch her glasses, and go for the new overnight permeable contacts now out on the market. She reached for her glass and then felt a hand on her butt. She turned and saw a man wink at her.

"Back off."

He held up his hands, but his grin remained.

Greta swallowed, suddenly becoming aware of the attention of other men in the bar. It made her uncomfortable. She was used to being overlooked. It had kept her safe. All the attention was unnerving. She thought of the man groping her and another staring at her chest. She had been naive to think she could be noticed by Vance and ignored by other men. Suddenly, she felt vulnerable—a target. All she could think about was how men were predators. They could be cruel, they could hurt you in many devious ways. She was scared. She wasn't used to being scared and she didn't know what to do. She didn't want to disappoint Vance. She wished she had his daughter's confidence or his ex-girlfriend, but they were used to being taken care of. Having someone to lean on. She only had herself. She had to keep herself safe.

She took a swig of the beer then left the half-empty glass on the counter and returned to Vance to grab her scarf. "I have to go."

He jumped up and grabbed her wrist. "You just got here."

She wrapped the jacket tightly around herself. "I know. I just have to go. Please," she said with rising panic. She didn't want to cause a scene.

His gaze locked into hers. "Did something just happen?"

Greta bit her lip then nodded.

His gaze darkened. "Point him out to me."

"No, I just want to go. Please let me go." He released her and she raced outside.

He followed her to the parking lot. "Tera, what's going on?"

"I'm so sorry," she said her voice trembling. "But I can't do this. All those men were looking at me."

"You can't blame them for looking at a beautiful woman."

"Beautiful?"

"Yes, you're beautiful."

Greta looked down at her clothes. "Maybe I should have worn something different."

Vance shook his head. "It's not just the clothes. It's you."

"No, it's the clothes and the makeup. I can't be this for you and this is the me you want."

"I want you just the way you are."

"Maybe you do, but your daughter doesn't and I know your family and friends will feel the same and they're right. I'm such a coward."

Vance sniffed. "You're the most courageous woman I know."

"You're wrong. I'm not courageous I'm terrified. I'm terrified that my mother will screw up again. And that my sister will get back on drugs, and my niece might follow their footsteps. I'm terrified of being attacked. I'm so pathetic. Most women want men to look and desire them, but it just scares me. One man touches my butt and all of a sudden I'm twelve years old again and a man—" She bit her lip.

Vance came towards her his voice soft. "A man what?"

Greta shook her head. "He touched me in a why a man shouldn't touch a child."

Vance swore, pulled her close and held her snugly.

"But I can't blame him. It's me. I'm afraid and I'm letting you down—"

Vance drew away and looked at her. "I never asked you to change. I don't need you to change. It's not about what anyone else thinks or says, it's about us. I like you just the way you are. Sure, I'd like to show you off looking this way. What guy doesn't want to show off a beautiful woman on his arm, but if that's not what you want, that's fine with me. I've lived so long caring about what other people think or said. I'm over that now. I just want to be with you."

It was at that moment Greta knew she loved him and the thought didn't scare her. Her grandmother was right. All men weren't beasts, and there were ones she could trust and love without fear. But she wasn't ready to express her feelings yet. She would use that love to make her strong. She took a deep, steadying breath. "Okay, let's go back in."

"You don't have to."

"Yes, I do." She took his hand. "Just don't let go."

He squeezed her hand and smiled. "I don't plan to."

Greta started to walk to the bar then stopped when Vance didn't move. "Come on."

He shook his head. "I don't want to go back inside." He pulled her to him and wrapped his arms around her waist. "I want you all to myself." His mouth covered hers and soon she forgot everything else.

"Your place or mine?" he whispered against her lips.

"Your place. Just give me a forty minute head start."

"Why so long?"

"I've got an idea."

VANCE WALKED into his apartment surprised to see it dark with just the glow of a purple light where Greta had thrown a pillowcase over the lampshades in the living room. There was a bottle of champagne, glitter and fake money on the table.

"Tera?"

"I'll be out in a minute. Sit down."

"What's all this for?"

"You."

"Me?"

"Yes."

Greta came into the living room dressed in a blue turquoise negligee that hugged all of her curves, black thigh-high silk stockings, and wearing a pair of open-toe, see-thru heels. A feather boa draped her shoulder, and to add some spice, a small diamond peeked out of her navel. "I want you to make it rain."

Vance began to grin, knowing that 'making it rain' referred to making the money fly in the air for a stripper. He pulled out his wallet. "I'll make it pour. What's your name?"

"My name?"

"Yes, you have to have a name."

"Umm...Sinful Pleasure."

Greta turned on the music and began to dance. Vance didn't take his eyes off her. She moved and gyrated her hips to the beat of the music. When she had stripped down to only a sequined garter belt and stockings, Vance made his final request. Although, by then all his 'money' was gone.

"I want a lap dance."

She paused thoughtful. "I don't know how to do that."

He bit back a laugh. "Make it up."

She straddled him. "You like this?"

"It's a good start. Where did you learn to move like that?"

"A woman has her ways. Actually, I was afraid you might not like it."

"Why not?"

"It's not exactly classy."

"You have all the class I need."

She reached in-between the cushions and pulled out a condom. "Would you find this more interesting?"

He swept her into his arms and stood. "Yes, I have a few moves of my own."

They made love that night with a deeper intimacy than they'd ever had before. Their bodies saying what words never could. Vance told her how gorgeous she was and how she'd stolen his heart; Greta shared how wonderful he was and how he'd changed her life.

"So when are we going to do this at your house?" he whispered against her neck, before placing a shivering trail of kisses across her chest.

"Someday," Greta breathed then lifted his head and covered his mouth with hers.

Vance met her passion with his own, wondering why "someday" sounded like never.

A MONTH later Vance looked up at his old high school then glanced over at his daughter who stood beside him in the parking lot. The cooling promise of autumn touched the late summer afternoon.

"What do you think?" he asked.

She frowned. "It's awful. Why did you bring me here?"

"Because it's part of my past. When your grandfather lost all of his money we were forced to live not far from here for a while and I went to this school. The environment wasn't what we were used to but we adjusted. Your uncle Kojo initially had a tough time fitting in. I fit in the only way I knew how. I played a role. I was brash, cocky and popular but scared inside. Tera on the other hand grew up around here and few things scared her. She made her way through some tough situations to become a success. No one looking at students from this school would have thought that one of them would become a top physicist. And the time I've spent with her have been the happiest of my life."

"Why are you telling me this?"

"Because I want you to respect her."

"I do."

"Did you talk to Tera about the way she looks and the type of clothes she should wear?"

Crystal hesitated. "Well...yes."

"Would you have done the same to Sylvie?"

"Sylvie didn't need help. You know that."

"So if Sylvie were to drive a car that you didn't think was cool you'd tell her about it?"

She frowned. "No, but cars are different."

"How?"

His daughter folded her arms, defensive. "I was only trying to help."

"That wasn't your place. Tera's a grown woman and if that's how she wants to dress that's fine with me."

"But she looks—"

"I like how she looks."

"Dad, be serious. Where can you take her? And grandma! Just you wait until she sees her. She'll be an easy target. Besides, I don't want a stepmother people will laugh at."

Vance raised a brow. "So, it's really about you."

"No, I really wanted to be a friend. She's so sweet and—"

"You can't like her the way she is?"

"I do like her, but—"

"But what?" he pressed when she stopped.

"I was almost jealous of the way you looked at her in that sports' bar. You've never looked at a woman that way before. You looked at her like she was the moon and stars. I'd always felt that that was my place. I know it sounds silly and childish. I liked our special bond, but with her you're someone I don't know."

"Crystal, with you I'm your father and that will never change. I love you and you're my heart. But with Tera, I can be a man. Completely myself. I don't have to play a role for her and I don't want her to play a role for me. I'm sorry if her appearance embarrasses you, but you're a grown woman now embarking on your own life. I want a life of my own too."

"I know, and I want that for you. I really do." She let her voice drop. "I didn't mean to make Tera feel bad."

"I know." Vance leaned against his car. "And you don't have to worry. She'll be able to handle your grandmother."

"How do you know?"

"Come over for dinner tonight and you'll see." His phone rang. Vance glanced down at the number. "Hello Tera."

"We'll have to postpone dinner," she said in a rush.

He straightened and gripped the phone. "Why? What's wrong?"

"Just business. Talk to you later." She hung up before he could say anything. Vance stared at the phone. He hadn't liked the sound of her voice. He called her back but got no reply. He'd stop by her house to see what was wrong.

CHAPTER SEVENTEEN

Greta could not have predicted that a simple knock on the door could put her life into another tailspin. She'd felt great that day. She had resumed going to rehearsals and had invited Vance to one of her concerts, where he'd promptly fallen asleep. But she was happy with her life and their relationship. So she'd been especially excited as she set dinner for Vance and Crystal, feeling proud that she was hosting guests for a meal in her newly remodeled house. But in an instant everything was gone.

Greta opened the door and stared at Brianna who had tears running down her face. She was now twenty-six, but obviously taking care of her mother had taken its toll and aged her. Her once smooth complexion looked dry and rough, and her hair looked brittle and lifeless, like it hadn't been washed for some time.

"What is it?" Greta asked. "Is it my mother causing trouble?"

"No, it's mine. You have to help me find her."

"What do you mean?"

"She hasn't come home in two days."

Greta felt her heart constrict. Marlene had been clean for months. The last time she'd spoken to her, she sounded fine. "What did Rita say?"

"She's with her boyfriend."

Greta clenched her hands into fists. Her mother didn't care about anyone, as long as she had a man, nothing else mattered. An hour later, after calling Vance to cancel dinner, Greta found herself in her third crack house that evening. It was a decrepit two-story wood house at the end of a dead end street. Peeling paint provided the only decoration in the sparsely furnished rooms, where bodies, some clothed, and some half-naked, where strewn everywhere on urine soaked mattresses.

Then she saw a half-nude body slumped in the corner: Marlene. Greta ran over to her and checked her pulse. It was weak but there. With Brianna's help they got Marlene in Greta's car and drove her to the closest emergency room. Greta didn't bother calling for an ambulance, because of where they were, she knew they wouldn't come or would take up to 45 minutes to an hour, and Marlene was in a bad shape. As Greta drove to the hospital, all she kept wondering was why. What had happened to all her sister's joys and hopes, the great adventure her fortune teller had told her about?

Seven hours later, Greta sat in her sister's hospital room with a tearful Brianna. Marlene had just survived an overdose —barely. When she looked over at her niece, who was absently rubbing her stomach, Greta saw something she hadn't noticed before, and it made her heart sink.

"Who's the father?" she asked gesturing to the small swell of her niece's belly. She looked about five months.

Brianna shrugged. "Just some guy."

Her sister had said the same thing years ago and likely her mother, Rita, had too. The men were always nameless and faceless. They were 'just some guy'. Greta knew there was no use scolding her. She'd tried to encourage her niece to get a college degree and choose a different path. She had even offered to pay her tuition. She'd wanted more for her niece, but Brianna was now a grown woman who could make her own choices. There was going to be another generation of the same. At least she'd waited until she was in her twenties, but Greta knew that raising a baby alone would still be a struggle. Greta turned from Brianna and looked at her sister. At that moment she felt she'd failed them both.

"How is she?" Rita asked coming into the room with a scruffy looking man close behind her.

Greta stood and looked at the man. "This is family only. You need to leave."

"I told them that he was my husband."

"That's a laugh, since you've never had one." Greta pointed to the man. "Go."

"She's in a mood," Rita said. She kissed the man. "See you later. Wait for me in the lounge." She waved him goodbye, then walked over to the bed. "How long will she have to stay?"

"She shouldn't even be in here," Greta said in a tight voice.

Rita shrugged. "It's not my fault she couldn't stay clean."

"You should have been looking out for her."

"How was I supposed to know what she was doing?"

"You know the signs, but you didn't care. She was doing great before you decided to leech off of her."

"I'm her mother."

"You don't know the meaning of the word. Did your new

boyfriend try to jack off on her again? Or maybe he was the one who got her back on drugs?"

"How come you're always blaming me? What about her?" She pointed to Brianna. "She got herself knocked up and that flipped Marlene out. She didn't know how she was going to handle another mouth to feed. She didn't want to call you because she didn't want to disappoint you. Where were you? How come you never stopped by our place?"

"I've been traveling for my job and dealing with my house repairs."

Rita rested a hand on her hip. "You just wanted to forget about us. That's all. You've got money. Why did you force Marlene to get a job and a place of her own?"

"I didn't force her to do anything. That's what she wanted."

"No, that's what you wanted. You wanted us out of your hair and you got it."

"No. Let me clarify. Marlene's over forty. It's time she stood on her own two feet."

"Right," Rita said with a sneer. "Because you know what's right for us. You were, no are, always telling us what to do. None of us can live up to your standards. "

Greta threw up her hands. Blame, blame, blame. It was always her fault. She was always failing them somehow and maybe her mother was right. "You're right. I'm done. I can't do this anymore. I won't tell you what to do anymore. I'm gone." Greta knew things were never going to change. Her niece would have her baby, maybe more. Her mother would continue having her men, and her sister would continue her struggle with drugs.

"That's right. Walk out on us. Your family. You are such a loser. You always wanted to get rid of us."

Greta glared at Rita. "No, just you."

WHEN SHE GOT in her car, Greta was too tired to cry. She didn't even cry on her drive home. She knew she couldn't just walk away from her sister, but she had to get away for awhile. She paused when she saw Vance's car in her driveway. She parked and shook her head when he got out.

"Not now," she said walking to her front door.

"Tera—"

Greta put her key in the lock. "I can't talk right now."

"What's going on?"

She spun around and faced him. "I can't see you anymore. Not because I don't want to be with you, but because I can't. My life will poison you. It's too much. It's too ugly. My family will suck the very life out of you and I don't want that to happen. I can't, no, I won't expose you and your daughter to what I have to deal with."

He shook his head. "I can face anything."

"Really?" Her voice cracked. "Can you face finding your sister half naked, in a coma, on a filthy floor in a crack house? Can you deal with your mother, who's now in her late-fifties, sleeping with another man you know won't last a year? Your niece is expecting a baby, after getting pregnant by 'some guy' looking to you for support? You've never had to face things like this and you shouldn't have to.

"Right now my sister is lying in the intensive care unit in a hospital bed, recovering from a drug overdose, with a whole bunch of tubes coming in and out of her. She'd been clean for months and my mother's is blaming me." She brushed tears aside, struggling against a wave of exhaustion that threatened to topple her. "I can't win with them. No matter how hard I try, I always fail."

"That's not true."

"Please, Vance." Her voice broke with misery. She seized the front of his shirt, held them in her fists and held his gaze, determined to make him understand. "I love you." She laughed bitterly. "I never thought I'd say that to a man, but I do." She rested her forehead against his chest, inhaling his scent and gaining strength from his presence. "I love you and I will not expose someone I love to this life." She reluctantly released her hold and met his eyes again. "Never." She turned to her door and opened it. "Things will never change, they will only get worse." She walked inside and then faced him, icy despair twisting her heart. "Goodbye." She started to close the door.

Vance stopped her with an intensity that surprised her. "I'm not saying goodbye."

"We have to."

"No, we don't. I don't care if things get worse." He stepped inside and closed the door behind him. "How come you feel responsible for taking care of everybody else, but won't let anyone take care of you? If you really love me, then you'll let me love you."

Greta hung her head, walked over to her couch and sat down. "I'm so tired and worn and broken. How can you love that?"

Vance sat down beside her and gathered her in his arms. "You're not broken, and if you're tired, then let me hold you up. Don't shut me out."

She looked up at him with hot tears burning her eyes. "I'd rather push you away than have you walk out on me. My grandmother couldn't cope. My mother, and my family are—"

"Not you. You've done well for yourself and you should be proud. I am. Nothing's going to tear me from your side."

Greta allowed herself to sink into the safety of his embrace and closed her eyes finally surrendering to the weight of her exhaustion. "And I don't want to let you go. Can you stay with me tonight?"

"I want to stay with you every night," Vance said, his voice deep and steady. "Will you let me?"

She nodded.

"You know what I'm asking you, right?"

Greta nodded again, and managed a smile. "I can feel your heart racing. Does the thought of marrying me make you that nervous?"

"No, it makes me extremely happy. The thought of spending the rest of my life with you...I can't put into words how I feel."

"I know," she whispered, then drifted off to sleep.

VANCE HELD a sleeping Greta in his arms, remembering their first night together months ago when he'd gotten a flat tire and she'd been attacked. She'd fallen asleep on his shoulder then, and he'd felt a sense of possessiveness that had surprised him. Now, the feeling was only stronger. He felt right, as if he were home.

She reminded him of his father. His father was a lot like Greta. Burdened by the need to be the savior to his large family in Ghana, but never feeling he was doing enough. He'd given hundreds of thousands of dollars to them over the years and Vance had just thought he was simple and foolish. He now understood it was more complicated. The bounds of family love and guilt all wrapped up together, creating chaos and uncertainty and strain in many people's lives. Especially for people like Greta, and his dad. For the first time in his life he was able to see his father in a new light, no longer as someone who was weak—but someone with integrity and his own sense of moral obligation.

He looked forward to introducing her to him. He didn't want her to feel alone. She had a new family now.

CHAPTER EIGHTEEN

"A drug addict?" his mother said outraged. You're going to marry a woman whose sister's a drug addict. Whose mother's a slut and whose niece is the same?"

Vance had called his father to discuss the problem with Greta but his father had insisted on having a family meeting instead. It was a tradition Vance hated, but couldn't avoid. Vance sat in his parents' fashionable living room and faced his mother, father, brother, daughter and sister-in-law. "Getting pregnant doesn't make you a slut," he said.

"With their kind, there's no distinction," his mother said. "Does she even know who the father is?" his mother asked.

Vance looked at his father then his mother. "I asked for your help not your judgment."

"He's right," his father said. "She will be family soon and it is our duty—"

"Don't talk to me about duty," his mother snapped. "I love you, but 'duty' is what nearly destroyed us. I won't see that happen again." She looked at Vance. "Why should we help them? This just proves that you should have stayed with

Sylvie. She didn't have all this drama and baggage. This Tera person just sees you as a meal ticket."

Kojo shook his head. "No, she doesn't and if we can help her I think we should."

His mother softened her tone. "You're so generous. I know you don't know how to be any other way. However, I'd expected more from your brother."

"Uncle is right," Crystal said. "I want to help too."

"Why haven't we met her yet?" his father asked.

"Dad was embarrassed," Crystal said.

Vance narrowed his eyes. "I was never embarrassed."

"Why would he be?" his father asked.

Crystal searched for words. "Because she's a bit...dowdy."

"Not anymore," Kojo said. "She looks amazing now."

"You will invite her for dinner," his father said.

"That's a good idea," his mother said with a smile. "Then we can see whether we should get involved or not."

Vance stood and walked to the door.

"Where are you going?" his mother asked surprised.

He spun around. "I am not going to have her face your prejudice or condescension. No, she's not Sylvie or Kara. She doesn't have the right name or connections, but I don't care. I needed help, but now I'm sorry I even asked. We'll handle this together, without you." He turned and headed for the front door.

His mother followed him. "Wait. Van. Please wait."

Vance took a deep breath then turned to her.

"I didn't know," she said with apology. "I didn't realize you loved this woman so much."

"Mom, I never knew I could feel this way. When she cries, it breaks my heart. When she laughs, I feel a joy I never imagined. I know I've disappointed you too many times to count—"

"No, you haven't. I've just been worried about you. I see myself in you. My parents were worried when I said I'd marry your father. It wasn't easy blending our cultures together and I know it won't be easy for you either."

"But you loved Dad."

"Yes. I still do."

"So you understand?"

His mother nodded then wrapped her arm through his. "Come back in."

SHE HAD to meet her of course. Bernice Lamine felt like a detective as she watched Greta leave her workplace and head for her car. She'd been following her for nearly a week, determined to see the kind of woman she was. Who was this woman who'd been able to wrap her son around her little finger? She'd first hired a private investigator who'd followed Greta and had reported that she was clean. Her routine was unremarkable. She basically went to work and then to her orchestra practice, aside from spending time with Van. The report had been costly and, unsatisfactory. Greta was smart and, from the photos the detective had shown her, beautiful, a dangerous combination. Her son liked to court trouble and Bernice knew that with a past like Greta's, there could be loads of it. She hoped not, but she wanted to make sure.

She lowered her head when she saw Greta headed in her direction, then jumped when something tapped on the passenger side window. She turned and saw Greta. Bernice hesitated then let the window down.

"Do you want to talk or just continue to follow me?" Greta

asked, gripping the front of her wool coat as a fierce autumn wind blew past.

Bernice sighed irritated that she'd been caught. She unlocked the door. "Get in."

Greta got in the passenger side then held out her hand. "It's a pleasure to meet you Mrs. Lamine."

Bernice shook her head, ignoring the outstretched hand. "Let's ignore the pretense. What do you really want with my son?"

Greta let her hand fall. "What do you think I want? I make enough money so I don't need his. And he is very attractive and has a great body but..." She smiled a little cruelly. "One can pay for things like that."

Bernice stiffened. "There's no need to be crude."

Greta shrugged. "I like to be honest. What questions did that investigator you hired to follow me not get answered?" Greta held up her hand when Bernice widened her eyes in surprise. "It's not his fault that I spotted him. When you grow up in the neighborhoods I did, you learn to always be on your guard. Let's just say, I'm extra sensitive and I know when a man is watching me." She sat back and clasped her hands together as if they were having a cordial drink. "I'm sure his report didn't reveal much about me. Aside from spending all the time I can with your son, I go to work and my orchestra practice. That's it. I have no secret addictions or another life. When it suits me, I can be a little rough around the edges, but I rarely need to now and—."

"Ms. Rodgers—"

"Please let me finish," Greta said in a polite, but firm voice.

Bernice bit her lip.

"I understand you love your son. I do too, so I'll make myself clear." She leaned forward and lowered her voice.

"Although Vance told me that you and your husband are going to help me deal with my family situation, I want you to know that I expect nothing from you. I understand you not wanting to be involved. If you want to come up with a lie to save face with Vance, that's fine."

Bernice met the defiance in Greta's eyes with a sense of unease then she caught a glimpse of pain and all her resistance fell away. "Are you saying you don't want our help?"

"Yes."

"What are you going to do?"

Greta lowered her gaze. "I don't know, but I'll think of something. I always do."

Bernice stared at the misery on the younger woman's face and finally realized how much Greta loved her son. How she wanted to carry this burden on her own, so that he wouldn't have to. She thought of what Vance had told her about Greta's family, especially her mother. She couldn't imagine the pain of having a mother like that. Greta needed to know what a mother's love could be and she was just the woman to show her. "You're being ridiculous."

Greta's head shot up. "What?"

"Of course we'll help you. And you are never to keep secrets like that from your husband. If there's something wrong, you are to handle them together. I had to learn that." She waved her words away. "But let's not talk about me. I already have an idea for your niece and we'll discuss your sister later." She reached out and held her hand. "I apologize."

"For what?"

"Not trusting you. I've just never seen my son like this and wondered who the woman was who'd taken his heart."

"I don't think he knows how much you care about him."

Bernice released her hand and shivered. "He'd be so angry if he knew what I've done. Please don't tell *ever* tell him."

Greta smiled. "I won't."

"And when you see me again, pretend that we've never met."

Greta's smile grew. "That's a promise."

Weeks later, Greta's conversation with Vance's mother felt like a dream, and she thought of it as she prepared to welcome his family over for dinner. She heard the sound of laughter and the clink of dishes as Kojo and Kara set the table, Minnie organized things in the living room, soon Crystal and Vance's parents would join them. She had a lot to be thankful for. His family had helped her in so many ways. Marlene was now in a long-term nursing facility. She wasn't going to get any better.

As a result of the overdose, she had suffered permanent brain damage that paralyzed her on one side and had taken away her ability to talk. After spending several days discussing her condition with Rita and Brianna, Greta made the decision to send her sister to the facility. From what the doctors had told her, Greta knew her sister would get the care she needed. Brianna was headed for Oklahoma where she had been invited to stay with Bernice's sister, who agreed to help her get into a trade school, that would give her the skills and a job she would need so that she could support her child.

Rita had disappeared, with another man, but Greta wasn't too concerned about her. Her mother was a like a rat, she always landed on her feet. While she felt her life was more settled, Greta knew she'd never know how to thank Vance's family enough for all they had done.

"Hmm, it smells good in here," Vance said, coming into the kitchen.

"It should," Greta said with a laugh. "You cooked most of it."

He opened the oven. "Yes, I'm good."

Greta playfully hit him with a dish towel. Living with him had been easier than she'd thought. At first, she'd worried about having him in her house, afraid that he'd try to dominate or take over, but they'd easily slipped into a relaxed relationship. He didn't mind cooking and she loved to clean, so they balanced each other. She looked forward to spending her life with him. She glanced down at her engagement ring, still remembering the moment when he'd slid it on her finger. "I still think it's too big."

He turned to see what she was referring to then looked away. "It's not too big. You're just not used to wearing jewelry."

"My wedding band better be smaller."

"Hmm." He pulled out some frozen dough from the fridge just as the doorbell rang. "Could you get that? My hands are full."

Greta draped the towel over her shoulder. "Saved by the bell, Bartie."

"Don't let anyone hear you call me that."

She mouthed the word Bartie as the backed out of the kitchen, then left to answer the door. When she did, Crystal stared at her, her eyes wide. "Tera?"

Greta laughed, knowing Crystal hadn't seen her since her makeover. Tonight she wore a yellow cashmere dress with her hair pulled up in a chignon. "Yes. It's me."

Crystal's gaze dropped to Greta's feet then rose to her hair. "You're so beautiful."

Greta led her into the sitting room. "You gave me the right nudge. Thank you."

She shook her head. "No, from the beginning Dad always knew you were beautiful. It just took the rest of us a while to see it."

"Speaking of your father, I'm sure he could use a hand in the kitchen."

Crystal kissed her on the cheek then left. Greta was about to close the door when she saw another car drive up. Bernice stepped, out then walked up to her with her arms opened.

"It's so good to meet you Mrs. Lamine," Greta said.

"Too bad Van isn't out here to see this performance," Bernice said under her breath.

"Let's keep it up, just in case someone is watching," Greta replied then she drew back. "I can't thank you enough—"

Bernice brushed her words aside. "You'll soon be family and that's what families do." She glanced around. "My husband is checking something in the car."

"Please go inside and make yourself comfortable," Greta said then turned her attention to the man coming up the driveway. Her smile froze on her face.

CHAPTER NINETEEN

"You're Vance's father?" Greta said, more to herself than to him, as the full picture came into place. Now she knew why Vance had once reminded her of him.

"Are you disappointed?"

"No. I'm so glad." Greta looked at the older man then hugged him. "I always wondered what happened to you."

He hugged her back. "You gave me the strength to go on. Because of you, we didn't go hungry."

Vance came to the door and looked at the two of them, confused. "What's going on?"

"My angel came back to me."

"Angel?"

"Yes. We met more than twenty years ago," his father said, wiping tears away. "You told me so much about her, but I had no idea it was my angel." He gestured to his wife. "Bernice, this is her. This is the girl I told you about all those years back. I never thought I'd see her again. But here she is. My daughter is home." He turned to Greta and started to clap and the others applauded.

Greta felt the wave of love that surrounded her. She looked at Vance's parents, Kojo, Kara and their baby girl, Crystal and Minnie, and knew she finally had the family she'd dreamt of. They gathered and ate and laughed for hours.

THAT EVENING, Vance and Greta lay in each other's arms, remembering the dinner with fondness. Vance rested his arm behind her head. "I guess we attended a reunion after all."

Greta's fingers lightly cascaded over his bare chest. "I liked this one much better than the first."

Vance covered her hand with his own. "If only I'd known back then."

Greta shook her head. "I'm glad you didn't."

He looked at her surprised. "Why not?"

"Because I didn't like you."

Vance laughed. "True, and I didn't like you either."

She turned and looked at him, amazed by the strength of her feelings for him. "But that's all different now."

His gaze melted into hers. "Yes."

"My grandmother was right."

"About what?"

About telling her to go to the reunion, to keep her heart open and encouraging her to give Vance another chance. But she didn't want to tell him all that. Instead she snaked her arms around him and held him tight, feeling safe in a way she never thought she'd be with a man. "Everything," she said then she kissed him and let her heart say the rest.

Table for Two

A Henson Series Novel

DARA GIRARD

NATIONAL BESTSELLING AUTHOR

ABOUT THE AUTHOR

Dara Girard, an award-winning, national bestselling author of more than forty novels, from romance to suspense, loves telling stories.

Born in the US to immigrant parents, Dara enjoys pulling from her Jamaican, British, Nigerian heritage and exposure to various cultures to bring what reviewers and fans call "vivid emotional stories" to life. She is best known for her popular Henson Series, the mysterious Clifton Sisters, and the fun Black Stockings Society.

You can write her at:
contactdara@daragirard.com
or
P.O. Box 10345
Silver Spring, MD 20914
If you'd like to receive a reply, please send a self-addressed stamped envelope.

Visit her website to sign up for her newsletter and get sneak peeks, monthly updates on new releases, and special offers.

For more information visit
www.daragirard.com